HELLION AT HEART

LEAGUE OF UNWEDDABLE GENTLEMEN, BOOK 2

TAMARA GILL

COPYRIGHT

Hellion at Heart
League of Unweddable Gentlemen, Book 2
Copyright © 2020 by Tamara Gill
Cover Art by Wicked Smart Designs
Editor Grace Bradley Editing
All rights reserved.

ISBN: 978-0-6487160-7-5

CHAPTER 1

Surrey 1813

*H*allie sat at the breakfast table with her papa, reading over the latest articles that had come out of Egypt and the wonderful finds of the ancient land that had been buried for thousands of years.

She sighed, looking out the window at the dreary, wet morning, dreaming of the heat, the sand and culture. Where spices floated in the air and invigorated the soul. Not like her life here in Surrey, where she did little except tend the garden and read in the library.

Her father cleared his throat, gaining her attention. "Hallie dear, there is something that I need to discuss with you. It is of great importance, so please let me finish before you say anything."

Hallie set down her paper, and turned to her papa. "Of course."

Her father, a gentleman, but one with limited land and fortune smiled a little and she frowned, wondering why he appeared so nervous. A light sheen of sweat formed on his forehead, and, picking up his napkin, he dabbed it away.

"My darling girl, this is not easy for me to tell you, and please know that I do this only because I have your best interest at heart."

She sat back in her chair, a hard knot forming in her stomach. "Of course," she managed, although she feared this conversation would be unlike any they had had before. Something was wrong, but what that was she partially didn't wish to know.

"I'm sending you away to a school in France. The Madame Dufour's Refining School for Girls is highly recommended and with your love of history, I think this will be good for you. You're never going to achieve your dreams by only reading the books in my library. All of which are sadly lacking and will be even more so in the months to come."

"You're sending me away? Why, Papa? I do not understand."

He sighed, reaching across the table to take her hand. His touch was warm and yet the idea of leaving Surrey, her papa, left her cold.

"I may have been born a gentleman, the fourth son of a baron, but simply being related to the aristocracy, no matter how distant, does not earn you funds. I have kept the house for as long as I could, but it was of no use and only yesterday I'm happy to say that I have sold it."

Hallie gasped, pulling her hand away. "You sold our home?"

Her father ignored her accusatory tone and nodded. "I did, and with the funds I have purchased myself a small cottage in Felday. It's a two-bedroom cottage that looks out onto the town square and it'll do us nicely I think. All our possessions that we can fit will come with us, the books also, and so I think we can make the cottage our own and be very comfortable there."

She shook her head, not believing what she was hearing. "Papa, our life is here. I was born in this very room. My last memories of Mama are here. Please, reconsider."

Her father pushed back his chair, scraping the feet against the floor. Hallie grimaced as he went to stand at the window, overlooking the hollyhocks and roses outside.

"Do you not think I know this, my dear? Do you not know that it broke my heart to sell our home, but it was either that, walk away with some funds, or walk away with nothing? I chose the former. The sale was profitable, and I have enough to keep me for the rest of my days, and to give you a small dowry along with your schooling in France."

He turned and strode over to her, pulling Hallie to stand. "You must promise me to use your time at school to better yourself. Arm yourself with so much knowledge that nothing and no one can stand in your way. That you will run with your smarts that I know you have and make a life from it. See the world, visit your beloved Egypt you're always reading about," he said, looking down at her article, "and live a full and happy life. Just as I and your mama always hoped for. You are always welcome at the cottage when you're home."

Hallie swallowed the lump in her throat, having never heard her father speak in such a way before. "I promise, Papa. I shall make you proud and before I go, together we'll ensure the cottage is just how we like it. Make it our new home away from this one."

Her papa pulled her into a fierce embrace and Hallie wrapped her arms about him, noticing for the first time how fragile and so much older he was than she realized. She squeezed him harder, wishing life to just halt a moment, to pause and stay as it was.

"I'm glad you said that, my dear. For I have old Farmer McKinnon coming tomorrow with his cart to help us shift. It'll be a busy two days."

Her father walked to the door, heading toward the foyer. Hallie followed him. "Two days. Why two days?" she asked.

He turned, smiling. "Because we have to be out of the house in two days. I suggest you finish breakfast and start packing."

Hallie stared after him, shutting her mouth with a snap. The house was not small, and the idea of packing, picking what they would keep and leave behind left her momentarily stunned. However would they do it with one house maid, a cook and one groomsman who also acted as their butler?

Shaking her head, but never one to shy away from hard work, Hallie called out to Maisie, her maid, for assistance. If they only had two days, then it would only take her two days to complete the relocation of their belongings. She rolled up her sleeves, heading toward the stairs. "I think I'll start with the guest bedroom first and work my way through," she said aloud to herself. Determined to hit her father's deadline and roll with the stones life throws at one's self, dodging accordingly.

CHAPTER 2

1817 New Years Day – Felday

It was the worst way in which to start the New Year. Hallie stood beside her carriage at the church yard gate, hating the fact that she was now an orphan. Even if she was three and twenty, her age did not change the fact that other than her school friends, she was alone in the world.

Snow fell about her, damp and miserable, and she looked up at the sky, wishing to be anywhere but here. Someplace hot so that her bones would no longer ache and her nose wouldn't feel like it was going to fall off.

The coachman helped her into the vehicle and she called for home. The small cottage that she would now close up and leave behind. Her father had always wanted her to live her life, use her education to explore, learn and enjoy the world that waited for her.

Now she would fulfil his wish and live. Not survive in this cold, wet England.

The journey into Felday was of short duration, and

Hallie stared out the window, thinking of her papa in his final days. By the time he'd passed, he'd been but a shell of his old self. A tumor in her father's kidney the doctor believed, the telltale yellowing skin and eyes of her father a sign that something was not right within his body.

Her only consolation through the ordeal was that he'd been happy. Her father accepted help when help was required, read and talked as they always had during the last few weeks. At times Hallie could even imagine he wasn't riddled with a disease, but those times were fleeting.

The carriage came to a quick halt and she slid off the seat, landing with an *oomph* on the floor. Scrambling to get up, Hallie heard a commotion outside and opened the door, wanting to see what the trouble was about herself.

She jumped out, the snow under foot crunching with each step. Hallie came about the front of the equipage to see a man, or better yet, a gentleman standing and talking to her driver. He was tall, his clothing much better made than her own, his greatcoat was cut to suit his muscular frame, and his legs were long and well-defined from hours on the back of a horse. Clean-shaven, his jaw was cutting, his lips full. A breath expelled at the sight of him. Heavens, Felday didn't sport men such as he. Hallie pulled her cloak about her, lest he see her own unfashionable clothes that had seen better years—her mourning gown that had been handed down from her mother.

"Oh, miss. I must impose on you to use your vehicle if you would not mind. Share it with you I should add. My friends, you see, have played a trick on me and have stolen my horse and I'm stuck out in the middle of nowhere not knowing which way to go."

Hallie stared at the Adonis as her mind scrambled to form a reply. He wore a fur cap and a large woollen scarf about his neck, but still she spied the hint of blond hair beneath. His eyes were wide and clear, a lovely dark shade of blue, his straight nose hinted at his breeding, not to mention his lips… They were full, fuller than perhaps her own, and for a moment Hallie thought she was looking at an angel sent to make her feel better on this sad day.

"Miss?" he queried again. "Do you think you could take me to the nearest town?" He hugged himself and she became aware of the chilling wind.

"Miss Evans, we dinna know who this man is. He could be a cutthroat, a highwayman." Her coachman pointed back toward Felday. "Walk in that direction and in an hour or so you'll make Felday."

"It'll be dark in half an hour," the gentleman said, turning back to Hallie. "Please, Miss Evans, if that is your name. Please may I hitch a ride?"

Hallie sighed. "What is your name, sir?"

He lifted his chin, bowing a little. "Arthur Howard at your service."

She lifted her brow, shaking her head a little. "Well, not really, it is I who's at your service, is it not?"

The Mr. Howard grinned and Hallie's stomach did a little absurd flip at the gesture. She adjusted her shawl, walking back to open the carriage door. "Back to Felday, John, and we'll drop Mr. Howard at the inn. I'm sure he can hire a horse from there on the morrow."

Hallie settled back on the squabs and pulled the carriage blanket to rest over her legs. Mr. Howard jumped in after her, shutting the door on the chill afternoon.

"Thank you again, Miss Evans for picking me up. I did have a horse, you understand, but I also have friends who think it quite a lark that they would leave with my said stead."

She studied him a moment, his articulation quite proper and correct. "Are you staying nearby?"

"I was staying at the Felday Manor and was returning to London with a group of friends when I stopped… Ah, I stopped for a moment and went into the woods and it was when I returned to the road that I found my horse and my friends gone."

Hallie shook her head at such absurdness. The man was not dressed to be left outdoors overnight and with the snow coming down quite heavily, he would've been dead by morning had he not reached Felday by foot.

"You are mistaken, Mr. Howard, for no friends would do such a thing, certainly not at this time of year."

He nodded, seemingly taking her point, before he sat back, crossing his arms over his chest in an effort to keep warm. "What brings you out on such a cold day, Miss Evans?" He smiled after his question and she pitied him her answer. Soon he would look at her with sorrow and sympathy like everyone else did in Felday village.

"I buried my father today, I'm returning home from the church."

His mouth popped open and she tore her gaze away from him to look outside. Soon, very soon she would be away from all this cold, this sadness and her life would start.

"Miss Evans, I'm so terribly sorry. Had I known I would never have intruded. You must forgive me. I am beyond regretful that my friends chose such an inappropriate time to play me a fool."

The carriage passed some outlying cottages of the county and Hallie turned back to the man who had turned as white as a ghost. "My father's passing was expected, Mr. Howard and he's out of misery now. Back in the hand of

God and I'm happy for that. You need not apologize. On a night such as this, it would've been unchristian of me to have left you on the road."

He reached across and clasped her hand. "Even so, as a man who has also lost both his parents, I understand how hard today must've been for you. I'm wretched that I intruded at such a time."

She shook her head, swiping at a tear that warmed her cheek. "Thank you. That is most kind, but do not trouble yourself. I live in Felday and was returning here in any case."

The carriage rocked to a halt, and Hallie looked out the window. The inn had two horses standing out the front and oddly three carriages were being unloaded. It wasn't usual to see so many people at the inn and Hallie frowned. "Mr. Howard, this is the inn in Felday, you had best go indoors and see if there is a room available. I wish you well," she said, holding out her hand to him. He picked it up and instead of shaking it, lifted it to his lips and kissed it gently.

A shiver stole over her skin and she smiled a little to hide her reaction to his touch.

"Do you have far to go this evening, Miss Evans?"

She pointed out the window across the town green to a little thatched-roof residence. "I live just over there, Mr. Howard. I think I shall find my way home well enough."

He nodded, reaching for the door. "Thank you again and may I wish you very well."

Hallie caught his eyes, drinking in his beauty as he closed the door behind him. When he went out of sight, Hallie sighed her relief. To remain calm in the face of such a handsome man was worthy of a prize. Her father would've thought it such a lark that a handsome stranger would arrive on the day she'd said her goodbyes to him. Even though in truth she'd said her goodbyes to her papa weeks ago.

And soon, very soon she'd say her goodbyes to England as well. And say hello to the Middle East and all that awaited her there. A life, as her father termed it.

A new start.

Egypt.

~

*L*ord Arthur Howard, Viscount Duncannon would murder his friends when he arrived back in London. Not for only taking off with his prized gelding that had cost him more than five hundred pounds, but because their stupidity had forced him into the company of a woman who had just buried her father.

Of all the despicable things for him to do, Arthur did not think he would ever better such an inconsiderate, lowly action if he tried.

He turned and watched the carriage as it pulled out on the small gravel road around the village green until it pulled up before the thatched-roof cottage across the way. The door of the home opened and closed and the carriage moved off. Arthur pushed open the door to the inn, satisfied that Miss Evans had returned home unharmed.

He walked into the front taproom and found a scene of utter chaos. The room was full to the brim with people, and the bartender and his wife looked to be running around as if they weren't sure what to do.

Arthur went up to the bar, calling out to the bartender who stood pouring two beers. "Sir, can I press you for a room? I need one for just one night if you will oblige me and show me where I may go."

The bartender, a tall, muscular-looking gentleman glanced at him and grinned. "Oh aye yes, and everyone else by the looks of it. I'm full up. You'll have to find some-where else to park ye ass tonight."

"I'm more than willing to sleep in the taproom if there is nowhere else."

"Taproom is full also. I have three carriages and two more wagons out the back. Full of the gentry and their staff who lost their way earlier today. I dinna have room for ya in here. You can sleep in the stables if ye like, but it'll cost ye a shilling."

"Thank you for your generosity," he said, doubting the man would hear the sarcasm in his tone. Arthur went back outdoors. It was now full dark, and he headed over to the stables that were down one side of the building. The chill air made his bones ache, and entering the barn, he sat on a nearby hay pile that was sheltered a little from the wind.

He sat there for a time, rubbing his hands together, but it was no good. He would never get to sleep and not only that, he doubted if he'd survive the night. Who knew Surrey could get so cold? How he would give anything right at this moment to be back in London, in his warm, comfortable home on Berkley square where he could stack his fire until it was roaring and no cold could seep into his bones.

He glanced out the stable doors, and from here he could see Miss Evan's little cottage, the candlelight flick-ering in the room behind her curtains. He stood, pacing and trying to warm his limbs. His mind whirred at imposing on her again. Arthur mumbled expletives. He could not disturb her for a second time in a matter of hours, especially after the day she had endured. He flexed his fingers, even in his kid-leather gloves, they were stiff and sore. His feet were tingling with lack of blood flow.

"Damn it," he swore. Arthur stood and started toward her residence. It was the most absurd, intrusive action he'd ever taken in his life, but it was either ask for shelter or freeze to death. Some men, strong men, may withstand a night in the stables, in the open without a fire or blanket, but he was not one of them.

He debated his choice all but a moment as he stood outside the green-painted threshold before rapping hard against the wood.

Miss Evans opened it, and now, without her black bonnet, black mourning gown and the large traveling cloak, she was unlike anything he'd ever beheld in his life.

She'd looked like a crow in the carriage before, but now… Now she was nothing of the kind.

He bowed, not sure what to do when one was at a loss for words, and so he fell back into that of a lord, remembering his manners when meeting a lady. "Miss Evans, I am throwing myself at your feet. Please pity me and allow me to stay here this evening. There are no rooms left at the inn, and having been sitting in the stable this past hour, I realize that I will not survive the night if I'm made to stay there."

Her eyes widened and she looked past him toward the inn before her attention snapped back to him. Her eyes, now that he could make out their color better, were a light green with the smallest fleck of blue through them. They were large, almond shaped, and her cheeks were the sweetest shade of pink. As for her hair, it was long and dark and he had the oddest feeling of wanting to see if it was as soft as it looked. Visions of it cascading over her bare shoulders in the throes of passion filled his mind and he cursed his wayward thoughts.

Miss Evans was not one of the many women in London who fell at his feet. She was an independent, honorable woman. His thoughts were dishonorable and not helpful.

At her continued silence, he said, "Please, Miss Evans. I will pay you handsomely if you will allow it."

His words caught her attention and she stepped back, allowing him to enter. "Very well, you may sleep before the fire, Mr. Howard."

Arthur headed straight for the fire, standing with his back to it and promising himself to kill his friends when he saw them again. "Thank you so very much. I shall pay you whatever you want, just name your price."

She raised her brow. "Any price, Mr. Howard? Are you a rich man?"

She came and sat on the settee before the fire and he chuckled. He was a wealthy gentleman, a viscount no less, and one with multiple estates and lands both in the country and London. She could name any price she chose and he'd pay it. Anything was better than freezing to death outside. For one, his grandmother would be very disappointed indeed should he die in Surrey before marrying one of the many heiresses of her choosing. A Duncannon married for wealth and connections. To freeze to death without fulfilling the family duty would be a catastrophe.

"Whatever you want, Miss Evans. The choice is yours."

She sat back on the lounge, and he looked down to see that she only had a pair of socks on her feet. The scene was awfully intimate, something a husband and wife may do late at night when all their staff were abed. She lifted her legs and placed them under her bottom and his lips twitched.

Arthur looked down at himself, his knee-high boots made by the best cobbler in London. His buckskin breeches and kid-leather gloves along with his riding jacket that was worth more than he would assume this small cottage cost. Not to mention his great coat and fur cap. He looked about, seeing a lot of books, but little else. The lounge Miss Evans sat upon was threadbare and worn, and the distinct smell of animal fat told him she did not use tallow candles.

"You have a lot of books here," he stated, matter-of-fact.

She glanced about. "Yes, they were my father's. We used to live in Felday House three miles from town. My father fell on hard times, and we were forced to move."

He frowned, not liking that so much pain and suffering had befallen the generous—and if he were not mistaken—intelligent woman before him. "I'm sorry, Miss Evans. That must have been a terrible blow to your family." He removed his gloves and slipped them into his pocket. "Another faux pas it would seem on my behalf since I was at Felday House just today. For what it is worth, the home was beautiful."

She shrugged. "It's been four years since I moved here, and I've been away at school most of that time. Soon I shall be going away again, closing up the cottage and starting my new life abroad."

"You are leaving?" Arthur pushed aside the odd twinge of regret he felt at hearing such news. Why would he be feeling such an emotion? It wasn't as if he knew her enough to be impacted by such information, and after today they would likely never meet again. And yet, the thought that he would never see her again made him melancholy. A state of being that he was not used to.

"I am. I've been offered a position as an assistant to Mr. Shelly, an Egyptologist from Cambridge University. He's traveling there to study the culture, the history and historical sites of course. I'm going to help him with those endeavours."

Arthur wasn't sure how to answer such a statement. To meet a woman who was going to embark on such a journey… Well it simply wasn't something that was done by the fairer sex. How splendid and intimidating at the same time.

"How extraordinary of you." He marvelled at her. "Are you not frightened? I would not think Egypt would be the easiest country to live, nor the coolest."

She laughed and her features lit up with the action. Not for the life of him could Arthur take his gaze from her pretty face and sweet nature. It was not every day one found someone on the road who would take a stranger into their home. Who was both beautiful and smart. Something told him the woman before him could hold an intelligent conversation that did not incorporate only discussions on current scandals or fashion.

"I should imagine not," she said. "But I think I shall like the warm. I'm so very sick of the cold." She shut her eyes, holding her face against the ceiling as if she already could feel the warmth of the sun on her skin. "I leave tomorrow for London to catch a ship the following day, so I had better like it, mustn't I?"

Arthur laughed. "I suppose you must." Warm now, he sat, but instead of sitting on the lone, leather-back chair to his left, he went and sat next to Miss Evans.

"May I know your given name, Miss Evans? You may call me Arthur if you please."

She turned and her inspection of him caused his blood to pump faster in his veins. How very odd. He'd never been so discombobulated with a woman before, and perhaps it was simply because the woman next to him was clever and soon to be more worldly than he as well.

"You may call me Hallie. Since you're staying here, I suppose it'll be all right." She leaned back on the settee and Arthur studied the fire.

"Have you thought about what you would like from me in payment for letting me stay here? I meant what I said when I said you may have whatever your heart desires."

Hallie pursed her lips and he swallowed. Damn it, he really needed to gain some manners. Next he'd be spouting love poetry at her feet if only she'd bestow him a kiss with her pretty mouth. He studied her profile a moment, his body tensing at the sight of her biting her plump bottom lip.

Bloody hell. He cringed. What a cad he was. A typical London rogue with no consideration for others.

"I do require some funds for my trip. I have very little, you see. Father did not leave very much, and although the cottage will be let while I'm away, I will not have access to those funds while in Egypt." She looked him over, and heat licked up his spine. "So for helping you today on the road, and this evening, I should like fifty pounds, if you will."

Fifty pounds… Well, she did play a hard bargain, but one he was willing to concede to. He nodded, but he in no way planned on leaving her such a small amount. The woman beside him deserved a whole lot more than that, and he would give her double before he walked away on the morrow.

"Consider it yours."

Her eyes brightened with pleasure. "Thank you, you're most kind. I had worried how I would pay for things while away. The position with Mr. Shelly pays very little, and your money will stop me from having to sell some household goods and valuables that I have here." She stood, folding a small rug she had draped over her legs and placing it on the settee. "I do not have a lot left from Papa you see, so I was sad to have to sell things to do what I know he wanted me to do in my life. How favourable that your friends would play such a trick on you after all. How opportune for me."

Arthur stood, sensing she was going to leave him alone. "The honor has been mine meeting you, Miss Evans...I mean, Hallie."

She smiled and once again the vision of her threw him off balance. How was a simple gesture leaving him floundering? "I will see you in the morning, Mr. Howard."

"Arthur, please," he said, wanting to hear his name one more time on her lips.

"Arthur..." she repeated, turning away.

Panic seized him that their time together was coming to an end. He reached out, stalling her. "Before you go, may we have a toast, in honor of your father?"

She seemed to think about it a moment, before she nodded. Arthur watched as she walked into her small kitchen just off the room, the sound of a cupboard opening and closing and the clinking of glasses telling him that she had agreed.

He threw her a small smile as she came back in with two glasses of red wine, handing him one. "To my father. A man of wisdom and kindness." She saluted and Arthur did the same.

"To Mr. Evans."

He watched as she sipped the wine, one single droplet sitting on her lip. Without thought, he reached out, wiping it away with his thumb. Her gaze tore to him, her eyes wide and shocked. He expected to see reproach in her vibrant green gaze, but he did not. If anything, her gaze dipped to his lips and the hairs on the back of his neck rose.

Hell, she was a beauty. A hidden treasure out in the middle of nowhere.

Having had his fair share of women, he could read the signs of need as well as anyone, and his body stirred at the need emanating from her. Arthur leaned forward, clasping her face. He stopped, but a whisper from her lips. Their breath mingled, the scent of her, warm and sweet, intoxicated his soul. Never had he ever met someone so unique. A woman so unlike those he was expected to marry. She was intoxicating.

"I'm going to kiss you, Hallie," he said, brushing his lips just the slightest against hers. As he expected, they were soft, pliant beneath his own.

What he did not expect, however, was for Hallie to kiss him back. No maidenly kiss, but a deep and thorough exploration of his mouth. The axis on which his world spun, tilted, sped up and whirled into unknown territory.

And he was lost with her in the middle of nowhere and happily so.

CHAPTER 3

London season 1824

*H*allie stood beside her closest friends in all the world at the Duke and Duchess of Whit-stone's opening ball for the 1824 London season. Everyone who was anyone had accepted the invitation to the duke's London home, which was rarely opened these days due to the fact the duke and duchess ran a successful horse racing estate. Such a large enterprise kept them busy most of the year.

But, as with people of such high rank, there was at times a duty to the peerage and His Grace had responsibilities at the House of Lords.

"So many people here. I'm sure we'll not all fit in this room if people keep arriving like they are."

Hallie absently nodded at her friend, Willow's observation, thinking she may be right. The duke and duchess had planned well however, and there were other options for their guests. A large supper room had been opened all evening, along with a card room that Hallie could see from where she stood was full of gentleman gamblers already.

The four terrace doors were ajar, allowing a little of the outdoors to venture inside. The night was mild and a stroll or conversation outside would not be uncomfortable. To be in England and a society that she had never circulated within before was odd. Hallie watched the *ton* at play, her mind always divided these days. Part of her life meant she had to take part in this world. Be seen due to her friendship with Ava, the Duchess of Whitstone. But her heart also remained with her son, who right at this time would be sound asleep if her cousin, who was bringing him up, had stuck to Hallie's routine.

Hallie checked her gown, thankful her friend Ava had loaned her a dress suitable for the evening. She had very little, other than an education and a cottage in Felday, which she could not return to at present since it was being leased. But one day she would return home with her son. The thought of her upcoming dig in Somerset would help in achieving that goal, and if she could secure more work that was similar, her financial independence would be secure.

A footman passed with a tray of champagne and she procured one, needing fortitude to face the evening, or at least one person who would be here that she'd not seen in three years, not since the night of the fire at Ava's estate.

Lord Duncannon. The very man that had used her home and then before she was even out of bed the next day, up and left without a word. He was a rake, and a charlatan, both charges she could lay at his door. That the Duke of Whitstone was best friends with the gentleman made little sense, and she had more than once asked Ava how it could be that her lovely, charming husband could be friends with such an ass.

Hallie shook her head, shamed over her actions that night in Felday. What she had done was so out of character it made one think she'd lost her mind. Quite possibly so, considering what she did.

"Oh, look, Ava and His Grace are opening the ball with a waltz. How lovely," Evie said, watching them with both adoration and longing.

A gentleman came up to Evie, another of their school friends who had been sent to France and asked her to dance. Hallie smiled, glad her friend was enjoying herself. Even if she only danced once this evening, it would be enough for Evie and make the ball one to remember in her opinion.

"Stop squeezing your champagne glass, Hallie. You'll break the crystal stem off."

Hallie relaxed her fingers around her glass, unaware she'd been holding it so tight. "Sorry, I'm tired is all. The voyage from Egypt was long and I do not believe I've yet acclimatized to the cooler weather. Nor have I slept very well since I have to have so many heavy blankets on me just to stop myself from freezing."

"Or," Willow said, inspecting her as if she were inspecting a new pair of kid leather gloves. "You're nervous."

Hallie frowned, turning back to watch the dancers and ignoring her friend. Had she somehow found out about her and her child? Not one of her friends knew of her disgrace and nor would they ever, not if she could manage it. Her son was happy and living with her cousin in Berkshire and he would be raised without the besmirch of bastard clouding his name if she could help it.

"What do I have to be nervous about? I'm about to start my own excavation in Somerset. I will be away from the dreadful *ton* and will have no one but myself to contend with for the next three months. I am the happiest woman here, I am sure," she lied, preferring to be with her little boy, but she could not. She had to earn money to ensure he was safe. Nothing else mattered.

"So if I were to tell you that Lord Duncannon was staring at you from across the ballroom floor, you would not react?"

Her legs went weak at the idea of him watching her. As best she could, she glanced at her friend, feigning indifference. "Tell me it isn't so." She did not want to see him and certainly she did not want to speak to him. Mr. Arthur Howard indeed. He had fooled her all those years ago, but he would not fool her again. It had been bad enough upon her arrival in London that she'd learned he was the newly appointed benefactor to the London Museum, the location that she was to deliver Mr. Shelly's latest finds from Egypt. It was the last of her duties with the Egyptologist, who had declared this to be his final dig in Egypt and so her employment under the gentleman had come to an end.

Thankfully the day she had delivered the artifacts, Lord Duncannon had been absent and she'd not been unfortunate enough to have to engage with him.

"He is, and he's been staring at you for the past five minutes." Willow threw her a curious glance. "Whatever happened between the two of you? He seems fond of you, but you're very cold and distant. It makes no sense. A marriage to such a great man would enable you to do whatever you pleased for the remainder of your life."

"Except it would not," Hallie retorted hotly. The Duncannons were renowned to marry well. Ava had mentioned it when she'd first returned from Egypt that the Duncannons placed wealth and position above all else. She was a mother to a young boy, an illegitimate one at that. She doubted Lord Duncannon would be so very favorable to her should he know her secret. "I'm too low on the social sphere to be anything but a plaything for his lordship." As she'd already found out. "Nor do I wish to become anyone's brood mare or hostess."

"Not necessarily. Take Ava for instance, she is still a successful businesswoman. Marrying the duke has not stopped her from running her racing estate."

"The duke is an exception to the rule." There were few men within this society who would allow such freedom for their wives. Ava had been lucky in her choice. Hallie would be lucky in her own way. She had her boy, and he was her future. She did not need a husband so long as she was able to continue to work and source an income.

Willow reached out, touching her arm. "I hope you do not wallow away from life simply because you've loved and lost, Hallie. I know you loved Omar but he's gone now, and there is a possibility that you'll find that kind of love again. Please do not keep running away to archaeological digs so you do not have to have a life. We want you to be happy. To marry and be loved."

Hallie sighed. How to tell your friends that that is not what she wanted. Not really. She would be perfectly content if she did not marry at all, so long as she could keep up her work and make her son happy and safe. England was littered with historical sites, Roman one's mostly, and they were just waiting to be explored. Having a husband would only intrude on finding them and she doubted there would be many men who would want an illegitimate child about their coattails. That is why she'd taken an advance to dig up an old Roman fort that was supposably located at Baron Bankes Estate near Dinnington Somerset.

It was the next best thing to being in Egypt and Roman sites often turned up coins, pottery, tiles and even weaponry. Plenty of interesting things to catalogue and hand over to the British museum once the dig was completed.

"If I could find a husband who would be content to travel, spend all day digging up dirt and had an open mind I would be well pleased. But you know as well as I that isn't a possibility. All the gentleman here are too busy with their many estates. I grant you there may be a few who would enjoy a little adventure, but they would soon tire of it."

"Lord Duncannon does not seem to have ever tired of you. He speaks of you all the time, so Ava has said. She did not push him on the subject of his interest of course, but it was definitely marked. You may have an admirer there."

Nerves fluttered in her stomach at the idea that his lordship had spoken about her to her friend. When they had been thrown together three years before during the fire at Ava's estate, she had just about swallowed her tongue in shock at seeing him again. After the night he spent at her cottage in Felday she had assumed never to see the gentleman again.

She had been so angry with him, had not been able to put their past behind them and move on as friends. During the time they were thrown together just prior to Ava and the duke's wedding, she'd barely spoken two words to him. He deserved less than that as it was.

So many things had changed since the night they first met.

She had met and fallen in love with Omar, had borne

his child. When she'd found out that he had died it was only a few weeks later that she'd come to realize she was with child. Luckily by then, the professor was wrapping up his expedition and they were soon to return home. Hallie had traveled with them as far as France and then she had made her own way home to Berkshire to her cousin's where she'd given birth and kept the notice of her child's birth secret from everyone she knew.

Shame washed through her that she had not married Omar like he'd wanted, regardless of what his family had thought. A mistake she would never be able to repair. She took a sip of her drink to quell the churning in her stomach.

"I do not care for his interest, as he well knows."

"Does he though, Hallie?" Willow asked as she looked out at the dancers before them. "He doesn't seem to."

Hallie wasn't sure if he knew exactly, but she'd certainly not shown interest in his lordship the last time they saw each other. An overwhelming urge to stomp her foot assailed her. If only he were not friends with the duke. If only she'd left him to freeze on the road in Surrey all those years ago she would not be suffering this introspection from her friend now, or the marked attention from the viscount across the room.

"I will remind him should he ask," she said. "I'm surprised he's not married in any case. Has he been linked to anyone romantically, do you know?" Why she asked she could not say, only that a man as handsome as the viscount was, left one to presume he would've been married off to a diamond of the *ton* years ago. It was certainly his family way of doing things after all.

Her friend watched her closely. Hallie fought to remain unaffected that one of the most sought-after men in

London was staring at her. "Why do I get the feeling that you know his lordship better than you're telling me? Come, Hallie, we're best friends. You can trust me."

She smiled, forcing herself to remain indifferent. "I do not know him well at all, I promise," she said. One night in a cottage together did not give her any more insight than anyone else spending an evening with him in company such as this.

It was silly to imagine otherwise.

～

*A*rthur stood at the opposite side of the room and drank in the vision that was Miss Hallie Evans. Damn, he'd not thought he could miss a woman as much as he'd missed her. Their one night in Surrey had left a permanent imprint in his mind and he would not stop until she was as carefree and sweet to him again, just as she was that cold winter's eve.

The following morning, after his one night in her arms, their farewell should have been bittersweet, with promises of seeing each other again. He'd woken early and had walked to the inn, wanting to order a carriage for both himself and Hallie to London. Hoping to be able to spend some time with her before she left England.

That his rascal friends had been at the inn, looking for him, had forced him into their carriage and taken him back to town without his approval or without him having given Miss Evans the money he promised her, still irked. He'd not run with them since that night, and he knew it was the reason she'd frozen him out whenever their paths crossed since. She'd ignored all his attempts of explanation and apologies.

He'd not heard or seen her again, not until the night that the Dowager Duchess of Whitstone had hosted a ball. Whitstone had been furious Ava had been excluded from the ball, and he remembered glancing up to see the one woman he'd thought forever lost to him, storming toward them like a warrior.

His legs had threatened to give out at the sight of her and it took some time before he could mumble anything coherent. Not that she'd wanted to hear a word from him, unless it was in response to her friend who had been treated unfairly by the duke's mother and as it happened, was in need of their help.

Arthur started toward her now, moving through the crush of bodies, all the while keeping a visual on her. *Hallie.* Even her name made his heart race. Tonight he would explain to her what happened, why he'd left and not returned. She had not wanted to hear anything from him when he'd seen her last, three years ago now, but no longer would he allow her to think the worst of him. She would know the truth and then she could decide if she wanted to continue to ignore his presence or at least be on congenial terms.

He bowed before her and smiled as her friend wished him good evening before she excused herself.

"Miss Evans, how lovely to see you here this evening. I did not know you would be in attendance."

She raised her brow, staring at him with a dismissing air. A little of his hope dissipated at her cold welcome. "I believe you knew I was back in London, Lord Duncannon. Of course I would attend my friend's ball."

He came to stand beside her and the scent of jasmine wafted from her skin and just like that he was transported back to Surrey and her little cottage. Did she still taste as sweet as the flower? He fisted his hands at his sides, knowing to think of her in such a way would not help his cause to make amends. To be friends at the very least.

"I hoped you would be here. I've wanted to speak to you for some time."

"Really? Do speak then, Mr. Howard…oh, please do excuse my mistake, Lord Duncannon," she amended.

He glanced at her, supposing he deserved that. Arthur noted the lovely golden hue to her skin, the light sheen of freckles across her nose that was not there when they had first met. She was a well-traveled, independent woman now, more so than when they'd first met. He marvelled at her ability to put him to shame. He'd done very little in the few years they had been apart, except try to escape the many marriage proposals his grandmother hounded him to make to women she thought appropriate. He could only imagine what life the woman before him had experienced abroad. Sadly, he had not traveled past the Scottish border, while she had seen part of the world people only ever dreamed about.

"I wanted to explain why I disappeared that morning in Surrey. It has been playing on my mind these many years."

She waved his concerns away, but refused to look at him. "That was a long time ago, my lord. Best I think that we leave it in the past where it belongs."

"Please let me explain, Miss Evans. I do want us to be friends since we share mutual ones and there will be many occasions that we shall be thrown together." All true of course, but it was not the only reason why he wanted her to like him. He enjoyed her, more than anyone he'd ever met before and he hated that she thought the worst of him, not when in truth, his leaving had not been his fault.

She did look at him then and the slight slumping of her shoulders told him she had succumbed to his plea. "Very well, tell me what happened to you that morning."

Relief poured through him that he had the opportunity to tell her the truth. "I went to the inn to order a carriage for London. I had every intention of returning to you, but my friends, the very ones that had left me on the road the night before had arrived and were looking for me. They bundled me into the carriage before I could explain and refused to stop until we reached London.

"I do not need to go into detail of how very in their cups they all were, but needless to say, upon arriving back in town I tried to track you down at the docks knowing you were heading there. I watched the Ariande push off from its moorings. I was late and I missed saying goodbye."

She watched him a moment and some of the fire burning in her eyes dimmed a little at his explanation. "Thank you for telling me, my lord. I'm pleased to hear you're not so fickle and rude as I had assumed."

"I am not, Miss Evans." He willed her to believe him. "I often thought of you. What you were doing and how you were acclimatizing to the warmer country. Her Grace said that you're home now having finished working for Mr. Shelly. Do you have any plans for your future?"

A small smile played about her lips, lips he'd dreamed about kissing again for years now. No matter how many women he'd taken to his bed, he wasn't fool enough not to notice that all of them were of similar coloring to Miss Evans. All had the same almond-shaped eyes, and pouty, full lips.

Not that it ever helped as none of them had her mind. None of them were her.

Hallie.

How could one night be so altering to one's life? It made no sense. He'd fought to move on from his little infatuation, but he'd failed at every turn. His grandmother despaired that he'd never marry, but he could not help but feel that Miss Evans was the other half to his soul. The one whom he should throw all family duty aside for and marry.

If only she would toss him a little crumb, a little bit of hope that she didn't loathe and distrust him as much as he feared.

"I'm going to be doing an excavation in Somerset. I leave tomorrow in fact. Baron Bankes is the gentleman who's hired me and I must admit I'm a little unsure of who he is, although the Duke of Whitstone has vouched for his character so I'm sure it'll be safe."

"I'm sure it will be," he said, knowing the baron well. "I find it fascinating that you had a dream, you worked hard and set out to achieve it. Not many women do what you've done, Miss Evans. You ought to write a book on it. I'm sure it would be very beneficial to young women who wish to follow in your footsteps."

She chuckled and the breath in his lungs seized having drawn one from her. "No, I shall continue to do what I love, for as long as I can and be content with that. But I suppose I'm fortunate to have had a father who allowed me to first educate myself and then travel abroad. Mr. Shelly was also liberally minded, so that helped as well."

Arthur smiled, warmth in his veins at her thawing toward him. "I should imagine so."

The musicians held up their instruments, the sounds of a minuet on their strings. Arthur held out his arm. "Will you do me the honor, Miss Evans?"

She stared at his arm a moment and he wasn't at all certain she would agree to his request. Relief poured through him when she placed her hand atop his arm. "Of course, thank you, my lord."

He led her out onto the floor as the music started. They took their places in the dance, others lining up beside them. At least this was a start, a new beginning to a history that had plagued him for years. He hated the fact she thought ill of him, especially when it was his friends who had played him that morning and severed his contact with Miss Evans before he'd made good on his promise and said his goodbyes.

Hallie, as he'd always think of her, was the one woman who had gotten away. She would not escape so easily a third time. He promised himself that.

~

*M*r. Robert Stewart stood at the side of the ballroom and watched as Miss Hallie Evans circulated about the room with her friends, one of whom was the Duchess of Whitstone. The bitch who had killed his cousin some years ago.

The duchess was almost impossible to get near these days, but her friend and the other woman who had been part of that tragic event were a lot easier to circulate near. If he could not gain his revenge on the duchess, he would hurt her friend Miss Evans just as the duchess had killed his cousin. He would be content with something similar.

Already tonight Miss Evans had walked past him numerous times. So close in fact that he had been able to reach out and touch her gown. She had not noticed of course, he was particularly good at being unnoticeable. Even so, having Lord Oakes as his cousin enabled him to circulate within this sphere, even after all that his cousin had done to so many people of rank.

The *ton* were fools. The lot of them he doubted could form one intelligent person between them. Apart from Miss Evans, who he understood to be a very clever, well-educated woman.

But not clever enough for her to hide all that she was.

A mother…

Not only that, but a mother to a bastard child of mixed race.

He took a sip of wine, watching her over the rim of his glass. The man whom she'd borne the child to was long dead, but his family was one of influence and power in Egypt, Cairo to be precise and he knew they would pay quite handsomely if they knew their eldest son had fathered a boy child.

In or out of wedlock.

His only question was, what was Miss Hallie Evans willing to pay to ensure he kept his mouth shut? He smirked at the thought of all the things he could make her do. Oh yes, this season would be pleasurable indeed.

For him at least.

CHAPTER 4

*H*allie looked about the room that she had been allocated. She had asked the maid who had directed her to the guest wing if maybe they had made a mistake. That she was certain being at the estate under the employment of Baron Bankes would mean he would wish her to be housed in the servants' quarters.

The maid had been adamant that wasn't the case, and had deposited her trunk, unpacked it quickly and efficiently and told her that should she require assistance to ring the bellpull and she would come immediately.

"Oh, and before I forget, Miss Evans. Dinner is at seven sharp if you wish to dine downstairs. However, you are welcome to eat in your room if you prefer." The servant bobbed a quick curtsy and was gone.

Hallie glanced about the bedchamber, the large, imposing double bed stood central in the room, and yet it was the only masculine piece of furniture she could see. Everything else was white, the cushions blue and pink, extremely feminine and pretty.

Not at all similar to how Hallie was in life, but she still

loved it. It reminded her of her mother's room from Felday House before they lost it.

She had been told upon arrival that the baron was not due to arrive for several days, but from tomorrow she had the help of two stable hands who would do any heavy lifting or digging she may require up at the Roman fort site.

Hallie untied her bonnet, laying it over a nearby chair, before walking to the window and looking out over the grounds. There were several hills that she could make out. From her correspondence with the baron, she knew one of the hills had once housed a Roman fort and there were reports that it too had a Roman family living there at the outpost at that time. The possibility that she may discover footings to old living dwellings, pottery, coins, or military equipment made the blood in her veins pump fast. The funds she would earn would also help in her plan for a secure future with her son.

The little cottage her father left her in Felday would be their home. The village people would believe her story that her husband had died, and her son would be accepted there. Her father had been a well-respected gentleman and she had always helped out at church or for anyone in need. They would support and protect her, she was sure. This position at the Baron's estate was another step toward a life she had to procure for her son. The next few weeks here in Somerset were going to be busy and exciting and she could not wait to get started.

Hallie sat down at the little desk, and picking up a quill and parchment, set out to write a letter to her cousin and son. They would be eager to learn of her safe arrival and all the things she planned to do while here.

≈

*T*he following day after breaking her fast, Hallie made her way out the servants' exit to where two stable hands—strong, young men of similar age she deduced—were waiting for her near the stable doors.

"Hello, I'm Miss Hallie Evans. It's a pleasure to meet you." She held out a hand and shook both of theirs in turn.

"I'm Greg and this is Bruce. A pleasure to be working with you, Miss Evans."

"Please, call me Hallie. We're going to be spending so much time together, I think it only makes sense that we forgo formalities."

They doffed their hats. "Of course, Miss... I mean, Miss Hallie."

Hallie gestured for them to lead the way. "If you would be so kind as to show me the locale of where this Roman fort was on the land I would be most appreciative."

The men picked up their wheelbarrows full of shovels and buckets and her equipment she'd had sent here a week past and started heading west of the property. The walk was uphill and they had to travel through a small woodland that circled the base of the hill before opening up to a cleared area of land. It took them half an hour to reach the top of the small hill and Hallie paused a moment to enjoy the view the height afforded her over Somerset.

From here she could see Baron Bankes's estate nestled in the gully below, it's glistening windows and sandstone walls standing out like a beacon about the green, lush lands. Slowly, Hallie turned, taking in the landscape of smaller hills, townships, rivers, and fields. A kaleidoscope of colors and one of the prettiest views to work by.

As much as she had loved Egypt, the heat, sand and people, she had missed her homeland. The green, lush land that was prone to rain would've been welcomed every now and then abroad, certainly during a lengthy summer where the temperatures soared. Hallie hadn't thought to miss it, the cold and damp, but at times she caught herself doing exactly that.

With the stable hands' help, she set up a small tent to the side of the hill, well away from where the supposed Roman remains would be excavated. The men chatted, telling her of the area, of what their families had once known to have stood here and what they thought the ruins had been used for. Within an hour everything was in place and ready for when they started their excavation the following day.

"I'm going to be sketching here for the remainder of the day, so you may return to the estate if you wish."

Greg wiped his brow, leaning on a long hammer he'd been using to bang in posts that marked the trench that was to be dug out. "Are you sure, Miss Hallie? We should probably not leave you all alone out here."

Bruce nodded, twisting his cap in his hands. "Greg is right, miss. We should not leave you here alone."

Hallie waved their concerns away, having worked with minimal supervision in Egypt. She was well used to being alone and out on dig sites. Egypt was a lot more dangerous than England and she had nothing to fear here. "I'll be fine and back at the estate for dinner. I have everything that I need here now and truly, I do not need to keep you from your work a moment longer," she added, seeing that neither man looked at all comfortable with her staying out on the hillside alone. "Unless there is some threat to my person that I'm not aware of. Is that so?" she asked.

Both men shook their heads, seemingly opposed to such an idea. "Of course not, Miss Hallie. We'll leave you be to your work."

Hallie pulled out her well-used, leather-bound sketch-book from her bag. She walked about the area in question that Baron Bankes had mentioned in his letters and glanced over the small sketches he had supplied.

There was a noticeable decline of the ground in certain areas that as a whole certainly looked like it could be where the outer building walls sat beneath the earth.

She picked up her small chair and sat, sketching the site, every stone that lay in the area now untouched for hundreds of years or even since the time that the fort supposedly sat here. For hours she lost herself in the drawings, moving about and drawing from different angles and degrees. At last she looked down at the many pages she'd filled in her sketchbook, happy with her progress.

A breeze blew across her skin and she glanced west, surprised to see the sun low on the horizon. She shivered at the evening air that started to settle over the land. Hallie stood, going into the tent and putting on her greatcoat, an article of clothing normally worn by men, but one she'd found indispensable when in England. After the years abroad in warmer climes, the damp, wet English weather was not something she was used to yet.

Before she lost light, Hallie packed up everything that could stay out on the site, stowing it away in the tent as best she could before starting back toward the estate. Lights were lit along the gravelled drive and the house was ablaze also, so very different to how the estate looked in the daylight.

She stopped just shy of where the woods ended and watched as carriages arrived before the double front doors, guests bundled out of the vehicles, their warn and wrinkled traveling apparel telling of their lengthy journeys.

Maybe the baron had arrived earlier than planned. Hallie skirted the woods, making her way around the back of the house, not wanting to be seen in her current attire and also too tired to attend any dinner or entertainment his lordship had planned for his guests.

Making the back servants' entrance she opened the door, scrubbing her hessian boots on the outside mat before stepping inside and closing the door on the cold night that had descended quicker than she'd thought it would. She would have to ensure the next time she finished up at the dig site that she gave herself plenty of time to return to the estate. She would hate to get lost and stuck outside in a location that she wasn't familiar with.

Hallie pulled off her gloves and stifled a scream as a shadowy presence leaning up against the wall stood straight and stepped into the light. She felt her mouth gape and she closed it, swallowing her surprise. "Lord Duncannon." Absently she remembered to curtsy and annoyingly she felt the heat of a blush rise on her cheeks.

She had not expected to see his lordship here. He'd certainly not mentioned traveling to Somerset when she told him of her plans. Whenever they were thrown together due to their mutual friendship with the Duke and Duchess of Whitstone it was awkward and hardly tolerable at best, and this chance meeting was no different.

"Miss Evans," he said, bowing. "Baron Bankes invited me to his estate for his month-long house party. I see you're already hard at work looking for historical artifacts."

His eyes took in her attire, his lips twitching when he noticed her breeches instead of a gown. His inspection of her prickled her pride and she raised her chin, well aware she was not the usual woman, certainly was not the type of lady that fluttered about in front of mirrors all day and cared for what was in the latest *La Belle Assemblée*. Women like those would suit Lord Duncannon and his esteemed family well.

"As you see," she said, moving past him and heading toward the servants' stairs. "Should you not be with your friends instead of pointing out my shortfalls, my lord?"

He ignored her question. "Are you not joining us this evening, Miss Evans?" he asked, turning but not following her.

Hallie threw him a dismissing glance, one she hoped he understood. She didn't want him following her coattails, nor did she particularly wish to be brought into the little upper-class party the baron was hosting. She may have a duchess as a best friend, but that was where her association with the *ton* started and ended. She was not part of that world and nor did she wish to be. If what had happened between them all those years ago proved men like his lordship were unworthy of her time, nothing would. "No, so if you'll excuse me I must return to my room. Goodnight, my lord."

~

*A*rthur chided himself for taking in her clothing and taking pleasure at the sight she made in the buckskin breeches and hessian boots. Not to mention her delightful shirt and jacket that accentuated her sweet form. Miss Evans disappeared up the servants' stairs and he rubbed a hand over his jaw. Just when he thought he was making progress with her, working toward being friends once again, he'd buggered it up by enjoying the sight of her instead of asking if her first day at the dig site was progressing well.

Idiot.

He inwardly groaned, the sight of her ass as it disappeared up the stairs embedded on his mind. A large whisky was what he needed and a cool bath. He shut his eyes a moment to gain some semblance of control. Always, whenever he was around her, the sensation that she was meant for him would not leave.

His family would never agree, she was poor after all, a bluestocking to her very core he had no doubt, but damn it all to hell, she was smart. An asset worth more than breeding and money combined. Especially since he needed neither in a wife. Not really. His family may have always thought these two things were priceless but he did not. Not after meeting Miss Evans all those years ago.

Now he wanted something entirely different.

Her.

He headed back into the drawing room, making his way over to Baron Bankes, his host for the month-long house party. One of the reasons why he'd accepted the invite was solely due to the fact that Hallie would be here. The baron had let it slip he'd hired her to excavate his Roman ruins and he could not come soon enough.

The baron summoned a footman for more wine, clapping Arthur on his shoulder in welcome. "How are you enjoying my home, my friend? I do believe there are some very fetching and available women here this month. Ladies that I know your grandmother would approve of." He chuckled. "We shall have a jolly time I'm sure."

Arthur smiled, taking in the room and finding little that tempted him. The one woman whom he'd never been able to get out of his mind was housed away upstairs and in no way tempted to join in with the activities downstairs.

A footman handed him a glass of red wine and Arthur took a satisfying sip, enjoying the oak and earthy flavors that bombarded his mouth from the well-aged beverage. "I do not see your historian here this evening. Is she here?" he queried, not wanting the baron to know he'd already seen her and her quick dismissal over joining them this evening.

The baron nodded, his cheeks ruddy from too much wine and the roaring fire behind him. Their host was a tall man, largely boned and with a jolly outlook on life. He was fond of the arts and history, which would explain why Miss Evans had been invited here to explore his ruins.

"Oh yes, she arrived yesterday. I sent word upstairs for her to attend whenever she was able, but I will not force her." Baron Bankes leaned in close. "Her father was a small gentleman farmer in Surrey, not a large landholder by any means, and I believe before he passed away they had lost their land and home due to debt and poor management. Miss Evans may not feel comfortable in our company, if you understand my meaning."

Arthur nodded, understanding only too well that she had to work for her living and in a line of business most unusual for a woman. "If you do not mind I would like to help her when I can out on the Roman dig site. As you know I'm the benefactor to the British Museum and historical finds are always most interesting to me."

"Oh yes, that tidbit quite slipped my mind. How are you finding the position?"

In truth Arthur had found the position uninspiring and with very little to attend to. To be the benefactor really only meant that when the museum required funds, he was obligated to open his purse. "Very satisfying," he lied, taking a sip of wine to lessen the sting of him lying to his friend's face. "Hence why I'm interested in Miss Evan's work."

Bankes nodded. "I will tell you something, but it must remain between us. I find the whole idea of a woman doing such a manual-labor, intensive job abhorrent, but the chit is very determined and seemed rather desperate for work. I could not turn her down." The baron laughed. "Let us not forget she's close to the Duchess of Whitstone and I must admit, I was swayed quite easily by her pretty face. One never knows, with such a woman under my roof, we may become better acquainted by the end of her stay." Bankes elbowed him and winked. "If you understand my meaning of course."

Arthur stared at him, unwilling to open his mouth lest he use it to shout expletives at the bastard for talking of Hallie in such a way. "She is a professional woman. I think your pretty words may be lost on her." He said the words in the nicest way he could without betraying the anger that simmered in his veins over what the baron had said. It would help no one, not even Hallie, if he allowed himself to say what he really wanted—that being for the man to stay the hell away from her unless he wanted someone feeding him with a spoon for the rest of his life.

"Bah, I think she would be willing. Hell, she spent years in Egypt without a chaperone. How virginal could she be?"

Arthur choked on his wine. "With all due respect, I know Miss Evans through the Duke and Duchess of Whitstone whom, might I remind you, are very fond of her. I do not think your speaking of her in such a way is becoming of you, nor respectful to Miss Evans and I must ask you to stop."

Bankes's eyes flew wide and his cheeks turned a deep,

ruddy color. "I do apologize if I have offended you, Lord Duncannon. I never meant to be offensive. I was merely teasing, you understand." His lordship smiled at another guest across the room. "If you would excuse me, I must attend my visitors."

Arthur watched him go, glad of the solitude for a moment. He needed to gain control of his temper, which had been awfully close to snapping at his lordship's crude innuendo toward Miss Evans. The baron would need watching, and so too would Miss Evans. Under no circumstances, no matter what she thought of him in particular, would he allow her to come to harm or be made fun of simply because of what she did for employment, or because her family had fallen on hard times.

He'd not stand for anything untoward or cruel.

CHAPTER 5

The following morning Hallie arrived on the dig site with five stable hands instead of the two like the day before. They waited for her on chairs they had carried up to the locale and stood when they spotted her arrival.

"Miss Hallie, we're ready to do whatever tasks that you bestow on us. The baron has given us his permission to work here for the day and so we're just waiting for your instruction to start."

"Wonderful, thank you so much," Hallie said, relief flowing through her that she had others up on site, and not two men, but five. It was pleasing that the baron found her employment here worth the men's time away from their duties at the estate. To have them here to help with the digging—a labor-intensive job she'd never been fond of would give them great results and quicker than expected.

"We will be digging a trench in the eastern corner of the site." She walked the men over to the location she meant and pointed to the small decline in the ground. "Under here I believe are the outlying walls of the fort. If you look on the area from a distance and higher up, the sinking of the earth is more prevalent and obvious. We will dig across it. A good three meters on either side and three meters long. The soil is to be piled together and if I may use two of your men here," she said, moving to where she wanted the excess dirt poured, "I'll have them sift through this soil to look for anything of historical value that we may have missed."

Greg doffed his cap, excitement gleaming in his eyes. Hallie supposed for men who normally only worked with horses this would be a little adventure in their life. The possibility of finding an ancient artifact was in her estimation better than shoveling horse shit all day. "Very good, Miss Hallie. We'll start on that right away."

Hallie went and put away her lunch and drink that cook had placed in a basket for her in the small tent. She pulled a smock she had made over her clothing to lessen the impact on her attire. Thankfully the men had not said anything about her trews and the leather, knee-high boots she wore along with a shirt and jacket. To take part in such digs was not possible if one had to wear a gown and she refused to be hindered in any clothing suitable for her sex. Stepping from the tent, she pulled on her broad-brimmed hat and picked up a small trowel from her crate of tools and went over to where the men were digging.

They worked all morning, only stopping for a bite to eat and drink around lunch. By the time late afternoon settled over the land the trench was a good ten inches deep and a few meters both wide and long. With the trench only on its first day Hallie could already see the old Roman foundations to the fort starting to emerge from their thousand-year grave.

The men having finished for the day packed up their

tools and offered to walk Hallie home. "I'll be along shortly. I need to draw today's findings and then I'll return to the estate. Thank you though," she said as they moved off down the hill, the mumble of their conversation fading along with the light.

Hallie pulled out her sketchbook, sat on a nearby chair and started to sketch. She lost herself in her drawing for a while, making sure to catalogue where little objects were laying and what she supposed they may be.

"I thought that I would walk you back to the estate, Miss Evans. A lady should not be out here alone."

Her hand stilled over the paper and she did not need to look up to see that it was Lord Duncannon. That he called her a lady made her teeth ache. She was no lady and in truth had never been. Certainly she never adhered to how a woman should go about society or anywhere for that matter. Her one night in his lordship's bed and her son born out of wedlock was proof of that.

"You do not need to do that, my lord. I'm more than capable of walking myself back to Baron Bankes's estate."

He came over to where she sat, and pulling up another chair nearby, he sat. "I know you are more than capable, but I wanted to come and see what the whole house party has been talking about all day. You're quite the latest *on dit*."

Hallie inwardly cringed. She didn't want to be anyone's talking point and nor did she want society looking in on her life. If they found out that she had birthed a child outside the sanctity of marriage, she would never work again. No one hired a strumpet. At least, that is what they'd call her.

"This is merely an archaeological dig, my lord. Unless we find something of significant historical value, I fail to see how the *ton* will be very much interested. As you can see," she said, gesturing to the stone wall soaking up the last of the summer rays after centuries of being buried, "this is merely stone. Not gold or jewels or some ancient artifact made of jade."

He glanced at the wall, a small smile playing about his mouth and she watched him a moment. Allowed herself to enjoy his handsome face. A face that from the moment she had picked him up on the road heading back into Felday she'd thought too good-looking to be noble. And that was exactly what he was.

A little voice chided her in her mind. *You were not exactly noble either…*

Her friend Ava had told her numerous stories of his lordship's escapades in town. The gentleman was a jokester and did not take anything serious. Why the day they had met, the man had been thrown out of his friend's carriage, and all for a lark.

Not that she had found it amusing. To be expelled out of a carriage to face the freezing temperatures of an English winter was the embodiment of stupid.

"Bankes mentioned it may be Roman. Do you think that to be the case after finally seeing some of the ruins?"

She nodded. "I do. Fourth century and from looking at the ground prior to starting this trench I do believe the theory that this was a fort is correct. It could turn out to be a villa, but it does not seem to be big enough to be one of them."

He looked at her and she fought not to fidget under his scrutiny. "You're a wealth of information, Miss Evans. I do not believe I've ever met a woman who is as educated as yourself."

"My education abroad was a good one, not to mention

working with Mr. Shelly in Egypt has supplied me untold information that you can only learn while on site. Text-books can only teach a person so much."

"May I help tomorrow?" he asked, pulling his gaze back to the half-dug trench. "I wanted to come up today, but I was waylaid." She sighed in relief at not having him look at her any longer. The man had the ability to unnerve her and she was much more her educated, quick-thinking self when he was gazing elsewhere.

"It's dirty work. I never took you for a man who liked to get his hands dirty." In fact, glancing at his gloveless hands, she noted his nails were well kept and perfectly clean. His skin soft and unmarked by the sun. Hallie glanced at her own chipped and dirty nails. The man was better kept than she, and she was a woman.

"I would like to. Between you and me, Miss Evans, a day up on the top of this hill digging in the dirt is a lot more enticing than being at the estate and having to pretend to want to be there."

She glanced at him. Why the sudden dislike of house parties and socializing? He was renowned to enjoy such events. Or at least, he used to be. Had he changed in the three years since she'd seen him last? "You may help if you wish, I will not stop you. But you need to dress with a little less finesse. I'd hate for you to ruin your superfine coat, not to mention those lovely cream breeches, my lord."

He glanced down at his pristine coat that was cut to his every measurement, the highly starched, perfectly tied cravat and buckskin breeches. He looked ready for a ball and not a day out in the woods or the tops of hills digging in the dirt.

He chuckled and the sound made her skin prickle in awareness. Would she ever be free of his pull? "I shall be dressed appropriately. What time do you leave? I shall walk with you."

"Be at the front doors by seven, my lord. We'll leave then."

⁓

*T*he following morning, Arthur was ready and waiting for Hallie when she stepped from the front doors, a heavy woollen cloak about her shoulders and what looked to be a knitted hat covering her hair and ears. Her cheeks were flushed pink from her morning toilette. She looked adorable and sweet enough to nibble on.

He shook his head at his recklessness. Here he was, about to trek to a hilltop and dig in dirt all day, and all so he could try to sway her to like him back. He was a besotted fool.

He could understand why she was wary of him and kept him at a distance. His reputation preceded him everywhere he went, and for years his family was known to be at a loss to his inaction toward marriage. Granted, some of the stories circulating town about his escapades were true. The friends he'd had the day he'd first met Hallie had given him a wild reputation, but he'd parted ways with them years ago. He was a different man now and he needed to show her that.

He caught little glimpses of her as they walked through the forest they passed through to make the dig site. Her freckled nose that was a little red from the cold morning. Her lack of self-awareness of how exquisite she was humbled him. Her skin had been kissed by the sun and she had a lovely golden hue, nothing like his pasty-white self who had never traveled out of England.

Her indifference to him quite literally drove him to distraction. She was one of the very few women who didn't seem interested in his person. A dilemma that kept him up half the night, but would please his family to no end.

The Duncannons were famous for grand matches, either in relation to wealth or position. He was a viscount and Miss Evens was a gentleman's daughter with little means. He had no doubt that Ava had told Hallie that his family would expect him to continue on the tradition of marrying well. That did not mean that at times, like today when he walked beside one of England's most intelligent, beautiful women that she did not tempt him to throw all of his family's expectations aside and do whatever the hell he wanted.

Namely choose her.

"What is the plan for today?" he asked, pulling his greatcoat closed farther to keep out the chill, morning air. Birdsong had commenced in the trees as the dawn broke and from here he could see a few deer grazing on the estate's lawns.

"We'll finish the trench and then start troweling the soil, looking for buried artifacts. I'll have the other men sift through the soil we dig out to ensure nothing is missed. I'm sure there will be some mosaic or cobblestone flooring buried. One never knows how elaborate these Roman ruins are going to be until we start digging deeper. Either way, I do hope to find some pieces which would at least date the fort and also give the baron some information about the site."

"I'm looking forward to being put to work," he said, rubbing his hands together.

She scoffed and he glanced at her. "You find such a statement amusing, Miss Evans?"

"A little. It will be the first time that I've seen a viscount wrist deep in mud." She threw him a small smile. A little crumb of kindness that he'd lap up. "Please, call me Hallie or Miss Hallie as the workmen do. We're about to dig in the dirt all day together, formalities be damned."

So bold and different. He stood in awe of her a moment, unsure of himself and how he should go about getting her to see him for more than what opinion she'd formed in her mind. He may know how to have a good time, certainly, he knew how to bring pleasure to the women he bedded, but that did not mean he could not be genuine or care for just one person.

He wanted her, he wasn't fool enough not to admit it. But she was also completely wrong for him. Opinionated and brash were not traits usually associated with a Duncannon bride. His family would never recover from such a shock. A Duncannon did not marry a commoner and certainly not one who enjoyed digging in the dirt all day long. History showed those who married into his family to be meek and sweet natured. Mollycoddled society princesses that even thinking about, made his teeth ache.

Arthur's lips twitched. Hallie was none of those things. He liked her in spite of this knowledge and as she jumped down into the trench, kneeling before an odd-shaped rock, oblivious to the dirt that stained her breeches, that affection grew. He could not picture his last mistress ever doing such a thing or those of his set back in London.

"Please call me Arthur in return," he said, kneeling down beside her and picking up his own tool to remove the soil about the circular stone in the ground. "What do you think this is?" he asked, ignoring the fact she remained businesslike and professional around him, while his own insides were in turmoil. To be this close to her, the sweet scent of rose in the wind, drove him to distraction.

"I believe it'll be a pot of some kind. Probably one that housed wine." She dug a little of the dirt away. "See," she pointed, "it's not rock, it's terracotta."

He ran his finger over the smooth edge, thinking of those who had used it last and when. "All these years it's been buried, and now here we are, bringing it back to the surface for others to see and enjoy."

She smiled at him, and his gut clenched at the pure joy he read in her vibrant, green eyes. This was the love of her life. Digging in the ground and finding hidden, lost worlds. He would have to work hard to make her see anything else other than the artifacts she was determined to find.

"My thoughts exactly, Arthur. I may make an archaeologist out of you yet."

He chuckled, doubtful of the fact, but enjoying his day out with her in any case. This life was not for him, but he could see the attraction to being so carefree. With his many estates this type of existence would never be a course open for his feet to tread.

"For today at least you will." He paused. "Now, let's see how big this pot actually is," he said, continuing to chip away the dirt from their find. "Anything to do with wine and you have my full attention."

CHAPTER 6

*T*he following evening Hallie was invited to dine and take part in after-dinner entertainments Baron Bankes was holding. She paced her room, continually going back to her wardrobe as if it would miraculously produce the latest designs from London for her to choose from. All of the gowns she had brought with her were pitiful and not at all suitable for dinner. Some she really ought to throw away, they were so tattered and worn.

She worked her bottom lip with her teeth. Maybe she could ask a maid to procure a dress from another female guest. If she asked nicely enough, maybe they would take pity on her and lend her a gown.

A light knock at the door sounded and she opened it, gasping at the sight of her friend. "Willow!" she said, pulling her into a fierce hug. "What on earth are you doing here?"

"We arrived this afternoon, you know my aunt the Viscountess Vance was invited and when Baron Bankes mentioned that you were working on his Roman fort excavation, well, I almost fell over myself to see you. Aunt wouldn't let me walk up the hill however, and I had to wait until tonight, but as soon as I'd heard you were home and preparing for dinner, I had to come see you."

Hallie pulled her into her room, marveling at Willow's beautiful gown. She was sent away to school in France just like her and their friends, and it was at Madame Dufour's Refining School for Girls that their friendship had been solidified. Of all of them, Willow had been the most fortunate. Her aunt had taken her in after her parents' deaths and her aunt happened to be wealthy, childless and titled.

Hallie devoured the sight of her friend, and the beautiful light-blue silk gown she wore, the long, elbow-length gloves and pretty pearl necklace. Willow was as beautiful inside as she was on the outside and a pang of hopelessness swamped her.

"You're not dressed yet, my dear." Willow walked over to her wardrobe, searching through her minuscule selection of gowns, a small frown settling between her eyes and marring her normally perfect visage. Willow turned toward her, shutting the wardrobe doors behind her with a decided snap. "Would you like to borrow one of my dresses? I have more than enough."

Hallie nodded in relief, only too willing to accept help. With the attire she had she would not be fit to be seen downstairs, nevertheless the dining room. "Thank you so much, dearest. I did not even think that I would be invited to dine and did not pack accordingly." Not to mention she was loathe to spend her funds on anything other than keeping Ammon clothed and well-kept at her cousin's. A new fashionable gown from London could keep her son clothed and fed for months on end, and so her attire had suffered and her lack of bother with it.

She supposed she would have to purchase at least one

gown if such situations like tonight came before her and there was no Willow Perry to save her the next time.

"Come, we'll go to my room and you can choose. I gather you've bathed already?"

"I have, and this dress is clean, although it's a day gown and not dinner appropriate, nor the latest in fashion."

Willow linked their arms and pulled her toward the door. "I have the perfect dress that'll suit your coloring. And you must tell me everything that you've been up to. I feel I did not see you enough in London and you escaped from there as soon as you were able. Please tell me that you're to stay in England from now on. I know Ava, Evie, and Molly along with I missed you dreadfully. What about your dig here? Have you been enjoying it?"

Hallie fought to remember every question Willow threw at her. She answered as best as she could, but also removed any mention of her child and the real reason she was so determined to escape London for employment. Not even Ava knew that she'd birthed a healthy and happy boy. Of course they knew of Omar, but not the child she'd birthed to him.

Nerves fluttered in her stomach at what her oldest and dearest friends would think of her should they find out she'd had a child out of wedlock, that her child was not only a bastard in society's eyes but also one of mixed race.

"You know London society has never suited me, and I wanted to visit my cousin before coming here. I'm going to stay in England for the foreseeable future, and this work, such as what I'm doing for Baron Bankes is what I want to do."

They made Willow's room and she ushered her inside, closing and locking the door behind her. "Well I for one am absolutely thrilled to have you here with me. I had thought this month-long house party would be a bore. Just my aunt catching up with her old friends, but it isn't so. Did you see Lord Duncannon is here? Has he seen you?"

She nodded, seating herself on the settee before the fire. Willow's room was more opulent than Hallie's, but that was to be expected when Willow was part of their set and Hallie was not. "He helped me out on the dig site yesterday in fact, but I have not seen him today. I believe some of the gentleman were riding about the estate today, getting themselves out of the house and into some fresh country air."

"Aunt said the same thing," Willow said, her words muffled as she searched through the abundance of gowns lining her wardrobe. "Ah, here it is. I found it."

Hallie gasped at the sight of the dress Willow held up before her. It was simply the most beautiful piece she'd ever beheld. The empire-style-cut gown was a deep emerald green silk with a cream, very fine tulle overlaying it. Decorative cream satin bands and lace embroidery about the hem and bodice completed the ensemble to perfection. She went over to where Willow held it up for her to inspect it, letting the silk and tulle run over her hand. It was so fine and soft, Hallie wasn't sure she should be allowed near such perfection.

"This will suit your coloring perfectly. It'll compliment your beautiful green eyes and lovely olive skin," Willow said, laying the gown on the bed and ringing for a maid. "I'll have my maid do up your hair for you and with this gown on you'll not feel the least out of place amongst the baron's guests."

Hallie clasped her friend's hands, so thankful she was here. Her eyes smarted with unshed tears and she sniffed. "I'm so glad you arrived, Willow. I had hoped to excuse myself from such entertainments. I certainly did not pack for anything other than clothes suitable for working in the fields. You have saved me this night, my friend."

Willow chuckled, bidding the maid entry when a light knock sounded on the door. "What are friends for if not for such things? Now sit, my dear and let Jane do her magic."

Hallie did as Willow asked and watched with fascination how Jane was able to set her hair to the latest style and with very little trouble. Tonight may not be so terrible after all.

~

*A*ll through dinner Arthur fought to keep his mind on the conversation that Lady Portman was whispering to his left. The young countess recently married was hard of hearing and spoke very lightly in fear that she would be too loud. She was a delightful dinner companion, and yet his attention kept being pulled to another part of the table where Hallie sat beside a gentleman he'd never met before, and also Lord Hood, an earl and old Eton school fellow. Both of them were rogues if their less-than-hidden infatuation with Hallie's lack of gown around her bodice area were any indication.

When he'd first seen her in the drawing room prior to dinner he'd almost choked on his own tongue. Of course he'd seen her in London at balls and parties, but after seeing her yesterday, grubby and disheveled out at her dig site, tonight she was perfection. A woman who turned heads and could hold her own conversations with her wit and quick mind.

He'd wanted to go up to her and speak to her, but she seemed to be a little of an oddity here at the party and everyone wanted to converse with the woman who was researching the Roman ruins on Bankes's property.

Arthur welcomed the distraction of his friend and marquess, Noah, Lord Capell who came and stood beside him.

"The archaeologist among us is dreadfully attractive I must say," Capell said, his attention coursing over Hallie.

Arthur narrowed his eyes at his lordship's observation before looking back at Hallie. Warmth spread along his skin when she laughed and spoke to her companions who flocked about her. "She has always been, as you well know. If only she would throw me a crumb or two of that kindness I'd be most pleased."

Capell glanced at him. "You like her in a romantic sense? You've never said so before."

"Not to you," he quipped, taking a sip of his drink. "There is something about her that I like and cannot shake. No matter how much I try to dismiss the idea, whenever I see her I'm right back there again, admiring her intelligence and easy manners. Wondering what a future would be like with her at my side." He chuckled at his own nonsense. "I apologize for my less-than-stimulating conversation."

Capell chuckled. "Never mind that. This conversation is indeed interesting, but even if Miss Evans is the Duchess of Whitstone's favorite friend, not even that will make her suitable for your family, Duncannon. You ought to look elsewhere for a bride."

The idea of doing such a thing irked, but it was what his family would want. "I know, but putting my family and their ingrained prejudices aside, she wants very little to do with me in any case. We get along well enough, and she's friendly when we're in the same social circle, but she is also distant." He didn't elaborate as to why that was so. His sleeping with her and then running off the next morning, or so she thought, was reason enough.

Capell clapped him on the shoulder. "Maybe, and I say this with the upmost respect to you, and our friendship, but maybe she doesn't see you in a romantic light. Even so, surely you're not looking to marry. We're not nine and twenty yet."

The idea of Hallie marrying someone else, of being with her husband alone and behind closed bedroom doors made his blood run cold. He hated the idea of her being with anyone else other than him, and so if he had to marry her to keep her for himself, he would.

Arthur digested that way of thinking for a moment. *Marriage.*

"You may be right." He glanced in her direction and caught her looking his way. His gaze hungrily took in her emerald silk gown and transparent tulle. Damn it she was beautiful, and that she was totally oblivious to the fact made her doubly so.

"Her little group of admirers seem to be moving on. If you wanted a chance to speak to her, may I suggest you go now."

Duncannon stepped toward her only to halt halfway when the gentleman who'd sat next to her at dinner came to her side and caught her attention. Arthur looked about for the footman carrying wine. He'd give her a moment with the gentleman and then he would talk to her. See if there was some way in which to create a comradeship with her that in time, he hoped would lead to more.

Perhaps even the state that in the past made him shudder in revulsion.

The marriage state.

CHAPTER 7

*R*obert sidled up next to Miss Evans and bestowed on her the best gentlemanly smile he could muster before the murdering wench. She inspected him, her gaze wary and he hoped he hadn't put her off at dinner when he spoke of the weather and the latest *on dit* floating around London. He didn't know really what one ought to talk about at these events, and certainly he did not want to talk to her at all if he could help it, but he did need to let her know that perhaps he knew more of her than she would like.

After all, his time here in Somerset was solely due to bring this bitch down and hurt the Duchess of Whitstone in turn through their friendship. To see both women fall from grace would be sweet indeed and his cousin would be pleased he'd accomplished revenge on them.

"Such a lovely party, do you not agree?" he asked, taking a glass of ratafia from a passing footman and taking a small sip of the sweet beverage. He caught Viscount Duncannon watching them with interest and he narrowed his eyes, making a mental note to be wary of the man. He did not need him sticking his nose in his business and halting his plan of bringing down the woman beside him.

"It certainly is," she replied, nothing more forthcoming.

A small smiled played about her sweet mouth as she took in the guests around them and he wondered if he could have a little fun with this woman before he brought her low. The idea of her mouth on him was not unpleasant and it would hurt her more should he play with her emotions a little before ripping away that footing from beneath her feet.

He leaned in toward her, closer than one ought. "Do you not ever wonder what secrets the guests at such events are hiding?" He took a sip of his drink, inwardly laughing as she stilled beside him. "Shall we guess as to what each guest may be keeping hidden? Secret lovers. Financial ruin. What else do you think we should include on our list, Miss Evans?"

"I should not know, Mr. Stewart. I've never taken the time to think about such things."

He met her gaze and did not miss the small flare of fear that entered her eyes. "Have you not?" he said, sighing for good measure. "Well, we shall have to think upon it I dare say. Do let me know if you come up with anything else. We shall make it our little game while we're here at Baron Bankes's estate. What say you?"

Miss Evans paled and Robert fought to keep a straight face. Oh, how delicious it was to torment her. She had supported and helped the duchess work out who was behind all the fires in Berkshire. Watched as his cousin died in her friend's home and did nothing to try and save him. He would bring this woman down, and through her the Duchess of Whitstone would be injured.

A young woman sat at the pianoforte and started to play a country jig. Robert held out his hand to Miss Evans. "Shall we dance? It looks like some of the other guests are partaking in the impromptu event."

She looked at his hand as if it were a snake, but shook her head, placing down her glass of champagne. "I'm sorry, no. I'm feeling unwell and will retire. Goodnight."

"Oh, I do hope you're feeling better soon, Miss Evans," he called after her as she fled. "Maybe tomorrow night we shall continue our little game. I will ensure the baron invites you to dine with us again."

She threw him a wobbly smile over her shoulder, but he could see the fear lurking in her dark, green orbs. "Goodnight, Mr. Stewart."

He bowed. "Goodnight, Miss Evans." *And sweet, untroubled dreams, my dear…*

~

*H*allie swallowed the bile that rose in her throat as she walked from the room, trying not to bring attention to herself. What Mr. Stewart had said had been so shocking and unexpected that it left her with little choice but to leave. To play a game, to question her on her thoughts on what others present may have hidden in their pasts made her question his motives. He was too bold, too amused by his game, for there not to be a nefarious reason he wanted to know.

Did he know of Omar? Had he learned of her child?

She fisted her hands at her sides to stop their shaking and as unhurried as she could, made her way back to her room. She would have to apologize to Baron Bankes tomorrow for her departure without saying a word, but not for a moment longer could she stay.

Hallie started to pull off the silk gloves Willow had lent her as she started down the long corridor to her room. Why would Mr. Stewart want to play such a game with her at all? His words told of someone trying to find out more information, and in this case, about her.

"Miss Evans," a voice called from behind.

Hallie shut her eyes at the sound of Lord Duncannon. Great, all she needed was for him to see and recognize her upset. He was too familiar with her, and able to read her like a book. She turned, attempted a look of pleasant interest that felt tight and unnatural to hold.

"Lord Duncannon," she answered, smiling a little. "Can I help you with anything?"

He stopped before her, his brow furrowed in concern. She considered him a moment, the sheer attractiveness that one man could possess didn't seem very fair in her estimation. Omar had been beautiful, dark-skinned, and his eyes the deepest brown with lashes that went on for days. Lord Duncannon was the opposite. His skin was fair, his eyes as blue as the ocean on a stormy day, his hair sun kissed and the color of wheat in the summer's sun.

She clutched at the gloves in her hand, aware that she'd started to undress before she'd made her room.

"Please do beg my pardon, but I could not help but notice you looked distressed when speaking to Mr. Stewart. You would let me know if he has insulted you in any way."

She nodded, swallowing the fear that the mention of the man brought forth in her. He had to know something, which made her wonder what was he going to do with that information and when.

"A sudden headache, my lord. Nothing more. I thank you for your concern."

He studied her a moment, his inspection thorough and a little skeptical. Hallie pasted on a smile, aware that if he were looking closely enough he would have seen through her like a pane of glass.

"If you're sure, Miss Evans." He frowned, seemingly fighting for the right words to say, or to ask if she were being truthful. "I will have a tisane brought up to you at once and a warming pan. The air is cold this evening."

She nodded, thankful for his kindness. After he'd left her in Felday, she had not thought he'd been capable of such emotion, but here he was, trying to comfort her without really knowing why. Hallie took in his finery, his strong jaw and aristocratic nose that could look down on people if he so chose. One thing he'd never done with her thankfully. Maybe he really had changed, or at least was trying to right the wrong he'd done to her all those years ago.

"I thank you," she said.

He nodded, stepping back. "Goodnight." Hallie watched him go, her mind whirring with what she should do. Not just about Mr. Stewart, but Lord Duncannon as well. Her secret was so very devastating, and there was a good chance that should anyone find out about her child she would never be offered the type of work she was now doing. To work in a great house as a lady's maid or a general housemaid could even prove difficult. No one liked to hire women who had not comported themselves in the manner in which was expected of them. Lord Duncannon may not look down on her now, but he would if he knew the truth. As much as she hoped that were not so, that he was honorable deep in his core, the fear that he too would turn against her would not shift.

She rubbed her brow, hopelessness swamping her. She could not let Mr. Stewart threaten her in such a way. Nor should she panic just yet. His game could have been just that, a silly little game that had hit home closer than he may know. For all she knew, the gentleman may not know anything at all.

Hallie opened her bedroom door and sank onto one of the leather chairs before the hearth. Tomorrow she would keep her wits about her, but carry on as if nothing had rattled her the night before. She would head up to the dig site at seven and continue her work and tomorrow evening she would attend dinner if she was invited and not scuttle off like a frightened bird before a cat.

Her future and that of her son's depended on her keeping a cool head and she would not fail him in this.

CHAPTER 8

The following day dawned with stormy, gray clouds and rain showers crossing the land. Hallie had fortunately made the excavation site before the first heavy shower passed over, and now with the ground damp, she helped the stable hands dig the last of the trench.

The hollow thud of horse's hooves on turf sounded and she turned to see Lord Duncannon pulling up a magnificent chestnut mount, his nose breathing out steam on the cool day and stomping one front hoof in protest at being halted on his morning run.

His lordship jumped off with little trouble and she admired the fact that he seemed so very good and accomplished at everything he did. His capable hands tied his mount to a nearby tree and he strolled toward her, his greatcoat billowing out from behind him like a cloak.

She glanced away, heat prickling her skin. Why she had this reaction with the gentleman every time she saw him was becoming exasperating. So what if he were the handsomest man she'd beheld in England? That did not mean she had to act or be silly over the notion. Nor did his being here mean that he was looking at her in any way romantic. He was, after all, the benefactor to the London Museum. If he did not take an interest in archaeological digs about England and abroad there would be something wrong.

"Lord Duncannon," she said, stepping out of the trench and walking over to him. "What brings you here today?"

He smiled down at her, pulling off his gloves. "I've come to help again of course." He strolled over to the tent and picked up the small trowel he was using the other day. "As I said before, I'd much prefer to be here than at the house party. They're playing charades and I do not feel like trying to figure out what or who people are. I'd much prefer to be here. With you," he added, his face serious all of a sudden.

Hallie reached out and pulled him to the side of the tent and out of vision from her workers. "My lord, I'm not certain why you're so very fascinated with the history of Baron Bankes's estate all of a sudden, but I must ensure that it's not because of me that you're here. We've known each other for some years, and well enough for me to speak plainly I think."

He raised his brow, crossing his arms over his chest. The action brought her vision to that part of his body. Her memory of their one night together many years before and what he felt like under her touch. Dear lord in heaven, she was going to hell.

"Do go on. I think I shall like to hear this opinion of yours."

She checked that the other men were out of hearing, all four of them still busy digging the trench. "What happened in Surrey will not happen again here if that is what you're hoping. Our night was a mistake. One that I regret and I hope you did not follow me here to Somerset in the hopes of having a bit of skirt to enjoy during the month-long house party."

A muscle twitched at his temple as he stared at her. "Is that what you think of me? That I'm only here to have you in my bed again."

The mention of being so once more sent an ache to settle deep in her core. She clutched her stomach, shaking her head, wishing that her body did not inwardly scream "yes" at the mention of exactly that. "I hope it is not. I was not myself that night and should never have propositioned you as I did. As you are well aware, I did not think we would see each other again. Certainly, I did not think that we would have friends in common."

He reached out, patting her shoulder and she narrowed her eyes. Disliking the condescending action. "Never fear, Hallie. I'm not here to seduce you, as much as I enjoyed our coming together the first time. No, I'm here to help as your friend and that is all. Your virtue is safe with me."

She studied him a moment hoping that were true, before walking back toward the trench. He was a complication she did not need, nor did she need him finding out she'd birthed a child by another man after being with him. He would think her a common whore who gave out her favors to anyone who passed her by. And that was not the truth.

Shame washed over her that she'd succumbed to his charm, good looks and too much wine that night in Surrey. That she had allowed herself to forget all her troubles and just give over to pleasure and passion to a man she thought never to see again. A reckless mistake she had regretted ever since.

Hallie rubbed the back of her neck, feeling his gaze

upon her as she made her way back over to the workmen. Lord Duncannon followed her and soon was working near where he had found the remnants of a wine barrel the day before last. Every so often she caught herself watching him, his little nuances like how he bit his lip when he was trying to be careful, or how a slip of hair kept falling over one of his eyes giving him a rakish appearance.

She snorted. Like he needed to look any more rakish. The man was a veritable sex god on mortal legs. That she knew just how godlike he could be in the heat of passion did not help either. Of how soft that hair was as he kissed her down her stomach, her hands clasping those golden locks as he dipped farther on her body.

Hallie pushed her shovel into the dirt with more gusto than was necessary. She was not attracted or interested in him in such a way. Not anymore.

Now she just had to convince her body of the fact.

~

*A*rthur could feel Hallie watching him. He'd be a liar if did not admit to liking having her eyes on him, watching him when she did not think anyone would notice. Today was the first time in years that they had broached the subject of their indiscretion in Surrey. He wasn't sure how it happened, and he supposed part of it was because she'd been so terribly sad when sitting next to him in the house that night. She'd just buried her father and he'd wanted to comfort her.

That comfort had spiralled into a hot and desperate coming together that had rattled him to the core. He'd left her bed early the next morning, walked to the inn to organize a carriage and had been practically abducted by his idiot friends.

It was any wonder she loathed him so much and did not offer the hand of friendship. He could not blame her, but he could try and change her mind about him. Tell her the truth.

He dug into the soil, looking out for anything that may surface and require delicate handling. Similar to Hallie, he would have to tread carefully around her. Earn her trust and see if they could move forward as friends and then possibly more.

His family would not like it, but then he wasn't controlled by them. From the moment he'd sat down in her small parlor in Felday he had felt a connection to her that he'd never felt with anyone else. An emotion he could not explain, and he knew, to his very core, that if he did not court her and see if what he hoped could be the start of something great, he'd regret it for the rest of his life.

His friends' actions and Hallie with her leaving had put paid to that idea. He shook his head. Hating the fact that they had missed an opportunity that may have been ever-lasting.

Hallie gasped and Arthur scrambled over to where she was digging. She started to remove more soil from the area she was excavating, taking her time to be careful. "Have you found something?"

"I think I have," she said. She smiled at him and his stomach clenched at the genuine pleasure written across her features. Hell, he loved seeing her happy, excited. "I think it may be gold. I caught a flash of color when I was digging."

He helped her remove soil from the area, and sure enough within a minute of further excavation the smooth top of a small, round-shaped artifact showed itself. They took their time removing the soil, and then within the hour Hallie had freed the buried piece of treasure and was holding it up before them. "I think this is a section of a legionnaire's helmet. How extraordinary."

Much like she was. He helped her to stand and for a moment they stared at the find. "The first of many great discoveries I hope."

She nodded, heading toward the tent and placing the item in a little box she had set up on a table. "Let us see what else this fort has to reveal, shall we?" she asked, slipping past him to go back to the trench.

"I'm right behind you, Miss Evans." Arthur settled down beside her. The remainder of the day did indeed sport new finds, other parts of the helmet and some arrowheads, although Hallie wasn't certain if they were from the fourth century or earlier.

Arthur contemplated his present circumstance. Should his grandmother see him now, Viscount Duncannon, boot deep in mud and digging in said mud for artifacts that no longer held any value to society, only the past. She would be appalled. And yet, never had he ever felt more alive and beneficial than he did right now next to Miss Evans. To be contributing to society, as small as it was.

CHAPTER 9

*H*allie sat in her room later that night after dinner where thankfully Mr. Stewart did not deign to bring up any more games that they should play regarding people's past. Her friend Willow sat across from her, quiet and reflective as she stared at the flames in the fire.

"Willow," she said, catching her attention. "There is something I need to tell you, all of our friends in fact, but since you're here, I wish to confide in you if I can."

Willow's brow furrowed and she turned toward her, giving her full attention. "Of course. You know that you can confide in me. I will never betray your trust."

Hallie clasped her stomach as nerves over admitting to her secret that she'd never told anyone other than her cousin. She was not certain how any of them would take the news, or if they would look down on her, scorn her for her choice. "There are two things really, and I'm uncertain what you'll think of me when I tell you."

Willow reached across the space that separated them

and clasped her hand. "I will never think less of you, no matter what you're about to tell me. I promise you that."

She hoped that was true, for to lose her friends over her secret would be unbearable. "You know how much I loved Omar, will always love him even though he's gone, but there is something that you do not know and I need to confide in someone before I shout it out at the top of my lungs for everyone to hear and be damned the consequences."

"Tell me what it is before I expire," Willow said, smiling a little.

Hallie took a calming breath and swallowed her fear. "Not long after Omar was killed I found out that I was carrying his child."

Willow gasped, wrenching back into her chair. "You were pregnant. What happened, Hallie?"

She stood, pacing back and forth between the hearth and her bed. "By then Mr. Shelly, the Egyptologist, was scheduled to leave and I jumped at the chance to return home. I needed to return home, to Berkshire, where my cousin lives and give birth. This all happened around the time that Ava lost her home to the fire. I went and visited her if you remember. Well, not that anyone knows it, but it was only a few weeks after giving birth to Ammon."

"You had a boy?" Willow asked, standing and coming over to her, clasping her hands. "You're a mother?"

Hallie nodded. "I am. He's the sweetest little boy, and my working here for the baron is so I can support him. I need positions like this so we'll be able to one day return to Surrcy, to my cottage in Felday and I'll never have to leave him again. But there is a problem with that."

"What problem?" Willow asked, frowning.

"Lord Duncannon problem," Hallie admitted. "I've

not been completely honest about his lordship either and after I tell you what happened many years ago I fear you'll think me a…"

"A what?" Willow clasped her shoulders to halt Hallie's pacing. "A what, Hallie?"

Hallie kept her attention on the fire, unable to look at her friend. "A whore," she admitted, shame washing through her that she'd been with two men in her life and both times married to neither of them. So unladylike even for a woman such as herself who thought women should have just as much freedom as men. Still, just like all the women of her acquaintance she was a product of her time and there were rules. Rules that she'd cast aside and now would have to pay the price for.

"You are not a whore. Tell me what happened, and please, stop pacing." Willow pulled her to sit back down before the hearth. "I want to know everything."

Hallie worked her bottom lip a moment before she said, "I first met Lord Duncannon by chance on the road to Felday, the day I buried Papa. He was cast off by his friends in a snowstorm and I gave him a lift to town so he may find a place to stay. But, due to the inclement weather, many people traveling through Surrey that day had halted in Felday for the night. There was no accommodation left in the town. Lord Duncannon asked if he could stay at my cottage and I couldn't see the harm in it and allowed him to." Hallie thought back on the night, the too many wines, the warm fire and cozy room, lit only by a single candle was a perfect situation for seduction and mistakes.

And oh boy, did she make one that night. The thought of his hands, strong and knowledgeable, certainly clever to make her even shiver to this day bombarded her mind. She let the memory take life in her mind as she told Willow all and everything that happened as if it were only yesterday.

"It started with a toast for papa, and spiraled out of control from there…"

~

Felday 1817

"I'm going to kiss you, Hallie," he'd said, brushing his lips just the slightest against hers. Without thought Hallie reached up and clasped his wicked, long locks and pulled him down for a kiss.

He moaned at her action and her body ached in places she'd not known could ache. What's more, Arthur kissed her back. He took her lips in a fierce way, and she scrambled to keep up with his desire.

She'd never done anything of the kind before, but a heady feeling came over her. A feeling that this was right and what she wanted, more than anything before leaving her home and starting a new life.

The action was scandalous of course, and when picking him up earlier today this was not how she thought her night would end, but in his arms, as his hand slid down hers, across her stomach and around to her bottom, nothing had ever felt so right.

"Are you sure?" he asked, kissing her throat and pulling the small ribbons on her dress apart, leaving the gown to gape at her neck.

Hallie nodded, kissing him again. "I'm sure," she gasped as his hand cupped her breast, his fingers finding her nipple and rolling it between his thumb and forefinger. Lightning shot through her veins and with a will of its own, her body purred against his like a feline seeking comfort.

Arthur stood, scooping her up in his arms and carrying her to her room. He lay her on the bed, following her down and kissing her, his intention as clear as her acquiescence.

"You're so beautiful." He rolled off her a little, lifting the hem of her dress, and pulled it upward over her body. Hallie sat up to allow him to take everything else off, and in her moonlit room she could see the need that burned in his gaze. He shucked off his breeches, his shirt his only attire, gaping at the neck and giving her a perfect view of his chiseled waist.

She reached over, taking the shirt in her hands and pulling it over his head. Hallie bit her lip at the sight that greeted her. His body was as lovely as his face, strong lines, taut and hers for the night.

Hallie ran her hand over the rippling muscles on his stomach, unable to stop her eyes from dipping to what stood erect between his legs. She reached down, running her finger along the tip and marveled at its perfection. "It's so soft and yet hard. I had no idea."

She felt his eyes upon her, and she looked up. "You're a virgin?" His words were breathless but controlled, and she nodded.

"Yes."

He frowned, his hand halting its path across her breasts.

"I don't want to stop," she said, moving over to him and wrapping her arms about his neck. "Show me what it's like before I leave all this behind. Just once I want to be with a man."

He pushed her hair off her face, clasping her jaw. "Are

you really sure? I don't want you to think that I took advantage of you tonight. This was not my intention when I came here. I need you to know that."

She kissed him, slowly and deeply, just as he had before and he wrenched her hard against his person. "I know you did not, but I want to. I really want to."

Arthur kissed her fiercely, falling back onto the bed. Hallie smiled through the embrace. Yes, this was what she wanted. This, all of this.

Her final memory before slipping off to sleep later that night, wrapped in his arms and hearing the thump of his heart against her ear, was of Arthur, and the perfect farewell gift he had given her. Multiple farewell gifts in fact.

Whatever next did the world have in store for her? She could not wait to find out.

~

*H*allie finished telling Willow of her one night with Lord Duncannon, minus most of the details that were for her memories only. Her friend's eyes were wide, her cheeks as red as a Scottish lass who had stood in the sun too long.

"Well," Willow said, breathlessly. "You know Lord Duncannon very well indeed."

Hallie nodded. "I did not know he was a lord at that time. He introduced himself as Mr. Howard. When I met him again at the Duchess of Whitstone's ball, the night of the fire at Ava's estate I learned who he really was. Not that it would have changed what happened that night in Surrey, but I certainly would have been more prepared than I was when we did meet again."

"Which you did not think would happen. Am I right?"

"That's right. But we have run into each other again and its awkward. I think he likes me," she admitted, meeting her friend's startled gaze. "What are you thinking? You look surprised by that."

Willow threw her a concerned glance. "I'm just worried, that is all. Living with my aunt has been informative and not always in a positive sense. These lords are not to be trusted, and while there are a few who can be, the Duke of Whitstone of course, but most of the men of my acquaintance are rogues and go through women like a cook goes through dishwater."

"Eww," Hallie said, not liking the idea that she was being looked upon as dishwater or a just one of many on Lord Duncannon's bedpost. But then, she ought to think this way, for it would most likely be true. He was a renowned rake. His family also strove for him to marry only the best. She was surprised he spoke to her at all, she was so far beneath him, in his family's estimation at least.

But he did speak to her, helped her at the dig site and was trying to make amends. Hallie could not fault him for that. He was sweet and caring toward her. He'd already slept with her, so there was no reason why he should continue to work on their friendship, unless he was being truthful and trying to make things right between them.

"You need to speak to him, tell him that what happened in Egypt. Explain that what occurred between you both will not happen again and that he should concentrate on more eligible women who are actually interested in his courtship." Willow studied her a moment and Hallie fought not to fidget under her inspection. "Unless you are wanting his attention."

Nerves fluttered in her stomach at the thought of him touching her. She stood and went over to her desk, pouring two glasses of wine, having had the maid who turned down her bed tonight procure her a bottle before she retired for the evening.

Hallie handed a glass to Willow and swallowed hers down in one go. "Of course I do not, and I have already told him that nothing further will occur between us. I have other things taking up my attention. I do not need a man to get in the way of my life. I've had my fill of all that. I cannot ever see anyone coming close to how Omar made me feel."

She slumped down in her chair, laying her head against its back, knowing what she'd just said was far from the truth. Lord Duncannon had made her feel things as well, not just Omar, but she could not voice such things. To hope where there was no hope was a mistake she could not make. That road led to heartbreak and it wasn't only herself to consider now. She had a son as well.

"I think if you're honest with him he will leave you alone. He is the Duke of Whitstone's closest friend. Whitstone would not be his friend if he was not honorable."

Hallie nodded, having thought the same. "We did talk of what happened in Surrey today, at the dig site. The way he spoke made me believe he wants more."

Willow chuckled, sipping her wine. "I'm sure he does, but that does not mean he's going to get one."

"Of course not," Hallie retorted, ignoring the fact her body seized at the idea of having his hands on her again. The first time had been quick but so very satisfying. After being with Omar she was well aware of what her body was capable of and what she liked. To take a lover was not an awful idea, but the risks were too high. To have any more children out of wedlock was not something she was willing to do. Not even for another night in his arms.

"I'm glad of it," Willow said, standing and clapping her shoulder as she walked past to place her glass back on Hallie's desk. "I will leave you now to get your rest, but do not worry so, Hallie. Be honest with Lord Duncannon and all will be well. You'll see, he will understand you're no longer looking for that type of relationship. Your son must take priority and he will respect your decision."

"Goodnight, Willow," Hallie said as her friend left her room, closing her door softly behind her. She stood and went back over to her desk, pouring herself another glass of wine. By the time she finished the bottle she was not only a little tipsy, she was also in need of another drink.

Perhaps the library had some whisky she could take up to her room. Hallie slipped on her dressing robe, and checking the passage outside her door noted no one about nor any noise from downstairs. A few sconces burned along the walls, lighting her way, but as she came to the staircase, she spied a footman below, slumped on his chair asleep, only a single candle burning in the entrance hall.

She slipped past him and started for the library, thankfully finding it empty. The decanter was full and she picked it up, wondering if taking that to her room would look a little bit extreme. Instead, she placed it back down, bending to look in the cupboard beneath. A bottle of red wine sat there along with an array of glasses. She picked up the wine and turned for the door, her steps a little uneven as she moved across the room, trying not to run into any furniture and make noise.

A quick look about the entrance produced only the sleeping servant who had not moved. Hallie ran past him, taking the stairs as fast as she could. When she made the passage that led to her room her nerves settled. The wine had made her warm and relaxed and after admitting her two biggest secrets tonight she was in need of fortification.

Thank heavens Willow had seemed to take the news well. Maybe her other friends would also when she told them, and she would have to tell them. And soon. She wanted to live with her child and she would no longer live hidden away, frightened of what everyone would think. If they chose to turn their backs, that was their cross to bear.

"Drinking alone is never a good thing, Miss Evans."

Hallie stifled a scream and fumbled with the bottle, almost dropping it. She glanced up and through the darkened hall spotted Lord Duncannon, similarly dressed to how he was the night they were in Surrey together. His buckskin breeches fitted him like a glove and his shirt gaped open, yet again tempting her to sin.

She shut her eyes, forcing away the visual. "Spying on me now, my lord. If you keep this up, I'll start to think you're obsessed with me."

He chuckled and pushed off from the wall, strolling with a relaxed air that reminded her of a predatory cat slinking after it's meal. "Oh, I admit that I'm obsessed with you, Miss Evans and enamoured, in awe and many other things. If only you would put me out of my misery and be with me. Always."

She gasped and slapped her hand over mouth, wondering if she had drunk too much tonight and was now imagining all of this. Surely not. "You tease," she said, calling his bluff and meeting him in the middle of the hall. Sandalwood wafted from his skin and this close she could see that he'd recently bathed. The idea of him neck deep in water, rubbing soap over his skin and washing his body caused a shiver to steal down her spine. She clutched the bottle of wine between her breasts in the hopes of stopping her hands reaching out and touching him.

To know what it felt like to be with Lord Duncannon, to be the sole recipient of the gentleman's attentions was not something to remove from one's mind without sheer force. A force made impossible by the foxed state she was currently in.

"I've never been more serious." He stepped closer still and his chest brushed hers. Her breath hitched and she dropped her hands to her sides, bottle dangling from one hand. Her heart beat so loud she was sure he would hear it.

"I told you earlier today that what happened between us was a mistake and one I'm not willing to repeat." She studied his jaw, a small shadow of stubble marring the normally perfect visage. Bloody damn it, he was just so good-looking and so sweet. Her fingers itched to slide up his chest and clasp his jaw, pull him down for a kiss. Allow him to seduce her to the thought of them, a future that would never eventuate. If she allowed this madness to commence it would only lead to heartache.

She could not countenance that.

"I want you, all of you, Hallie. I have since the day you offered me a ride in Surrey. Did you not feel it also?"

She shut her eyes, willing the emotions that he wrought up in her to subside. To leave and never come back. He wasn't for her. If her lineage wasn't enough to exclude her to be anything to him, her actions in Egypt and the son she'd borne out of wedlock certainly would put paid to that notion.

"It makes no difference what I feel. We can only ever be friends." She started back to her room, needing to be away from him and all that he offered. To be loved by the

Viscount Duncannon meant security and safety, both for her and her son. But it was a fickle dream. As soon as he knew the truth of her situation he would run for the hills. No man wanted to bring up another man's child. Especially if that child had not been born in wedlock.

He pulled her to a stop, whipping her around to look at him. "Why are you fighting this? I know you feel something for me, so if it's not too much trouble I'd like you to stop pushing me away. Can you do that?"

She ripped her arm free, glaring at him. Hating him for being so honest. It would be so much easier to deny him if he were not so sweet. "I do not feel anything for you, my lord. I'm sorry to disappoint you, but that is the truth."

"Really?" he said, a sarcastic tilt to his mouth. "Why do I not believe that?" he whispered, leaning close and tempting her with his lips.

She bit her bottom lip, forcing her gaze away from his face. "You should. It's the truth. Goodnight." Hallie walked back to her room, the need to run almost impossible to deny. He didn't follow her this time and she was thankful for it. She wasn't sure she could deny him a second time. Not with her mind fuzzy with too much wine and also his own persuasive self.

His tempting words for a life with her.

CHAPTER 10

*H*allie was late to the site the following day, a headache thumping hard at her temples. She watched from the safety of the tent as the men continued to dig, trowel, and sift through the soil in and out of the trench. She sketched some of the artifacts that had been found, and also the site itself, content with that line of work instead of the more manual-intensive jobs she would normally do.

No one wanted to see a woman cast up her accounts.

Lord Duncannon had not visited her on the site and she ignored the fact that his not being there made her stomach churn in an unpleasant way. Or it could be churning because of all the wine she'd imbibed the night before, having had several more glasses after leaving Arthur. Thankfully she'd fallen asleep and had not gone to his room to allow him to further their acquaintance.

Hallie rubbed her brow, her mind not as sharp or clear as it normally was. She would not drink again, she promised herself. No more drinking her worries into submission. She would face her fears and her life just as her father brought her up to face them. Head on and with her chin raised.

"Here you are," a deep, gravelly voice said before a head popped between the tent flaps.

Her heart gave a jump at the sight of him, all his blond, godlike features and a smile that would seduce a nun. "What are you doing here?" she asked, standing, clutching her sketchbook to her chest as if to ward him off like paper armor.

"Coming to see if you've changed your mind."

"I haven't," she retorted, stepping away to place the small work table between them.

He strolled into the tent, one hand idly running across the table top as he walked toward her. "Maybe you need a reminder of how very good it can be between us."

Hallie shut her eyes, no reminder necessary. She could remember every second of their time together in Surrey. Every touch and look, the way his lips took hers, demanding and yet, soft and supple.

"I know you're lying, my dear. Come, kiss me."

She halted and he continued to stroll about the table, catching up to her. "Kiss me, Hallie. If after our kiss you still do not feel anything for me other than friendship, I shall never bother you again. I promise," he said, making the sign of a cross over his chest.

Hallie pursed her lips, debating the offer. It would certainly allow her to tell him at least that his kiss did not affect her, even if it did.

"Very well, you may kiss me. Once. And that is all."

"And that is quite enough, I assure you," he said, quickly, hoisting her into his arms and taking her lips without hesitation.

~

The moment Arthur's lips touched Hallie's he knew what it was to feel right. The woman in his arms was his other half in this world. He was sure of it. She melted against him and he deepened the embrace, wanting to show her all that she made him feel, and she made him feel so damn much.

More than he had ever felt with anyone else. He'd known it the moment he'd touched her in Surrey she was different. His soul knew she was the one. Now, he had to convince her of the fact and his family, who would not be impressed that he was marrying a woman out of the sphere in which they circulated.

"You're so sweet," he said, lifting her to set her on her workbench. She gasped at the action and he took the opportunity to kiss her long and deep. His body roared to life when she kissed him back with as much passion as he remembered, spiking his need of her. It had been so very long since he'd been with a woman and especially a woman that made him feel so much more than just running through the motions of seduction.

He wanted more for Hallie. Wanted to make her happy both in these situations and in everyday life. He wanted to give her a home, security and, god willing, children.

Her hands clutched at his shoulders before slipping around his neck, pulling him close. He could feel her breasts rising with each breath against his chest and he ached to cup them. Arthur kept his hands on her waist, demanding them to stay put and not move. Not to push her too far. He needed her in his life, not to run away in fear.

Her tongue slipped against his and he growled. Damn

it she tempted him like a siren's call. He stepped closer still, placing him hard against her body. A shame they both were fully clothed. He undulated against her sex, eliciting a gasp from her. Her leg wrapped about his, pulling him closer still.

Arthur's cock was as hard as a rod and he pushed against her sex, the action teased him and he fought not to spill in his pants like a green lad. Her raspy intake of breaths did odd things to him, and he increased his pace. Had anyone walked in, it would have appeared as if they were rutting like two wild beasts. He wanted to have her again, dreamed about it often for years, if he were honest with himself.

The sound of men's laughter outside the tent pulled him back to his wits and he wrenched out of her arms, stepping away. She jumped off the table, holding it for support just as Bruce pushed up the tent flaps and entered, taking his cap off when he spied them.

"Miss Hallie, we've found another gold artifact. Did you want to have a look at it before we trowel farther into the ground?"

Arthur watched as she fought to regain her composure. She checked her hair, and then looking about, grabbed her woollen cap she was fond of wearing and, slipping it on her head, walked out the tent without a word.

Arthur leaned upon the table, taking deep, calming breaths. Damn it all to hell the one kiss he'd asked for had progressed too fast that even now his head swam. He stared after her, hoping she would not dismiss him after his slip of etiquette.

There was something between them, and he needed to find out what that was. He had a sneaking suspicion that it was something akin to what his good friend the Duke of Whitstone felt for his wife.

He ran a hand through his hair, checking his clothing before heading outside to join Hallie and her workers at the trench. Surely after a kiss such as the one they just shared she would agree that they had something special. Something that only came around once in one's life.

Something to hold on to and not throw away, no matter the obstacles.

～

Later that night Hallie sat in the drawing room, listening to Willow talk of her day and that her aunt had given her approval to visit her dig site on the morrow. All of her friends' words were lost on her as her attention had been captivated by the very deadly and seductive Lord Duncannon, who spoke with a group of gentlemen across the room, including Baron Bankes.

After losing Omar she had sworn not to become affected or drawn into the games of men. But then, Lord Duncannon was unlike most men. That she'd known him before she left for Egypt also was a factor. Even then, when she hardly knew the gentleman, she had felt a connection to him. Lust, more than anything. Of that she was certain now that she knew what that emotion was.

And she was feeling that emotion again and more. A sentiment she didn't want to delve into too much right at the moment. To walk that path meant risking her heart, and she wasn't sure she could survive it breaking a second time.

She inwardly cursed at being weak. She needed to be strong, for her own moral compass and for her son. To be with a man again was a risk and she was certain that even as deadly sexy as his lordship was, he was not worth that price.

He laughed at something the baron said, and her heart skipped a beat. She sighed, maybe he was worth that price…

"Hallie? Have you heard a word that I said to you?"

Hallie turned to Willow and fought to recall what her friend had been telling her. Something about lace… "I'm sorry, Willow. I was wool-gathering."

"You were not," her friend retorted. "You were watching a certain blond god across the room."

Heat bloomed on her cheeks and she shook her head, physically dismissing the idea even though her mind shouted, *yes, yes she was watching him and enjoying every moment of it.* "Of course I was not. I was merely taking in the guests, that is all. Lady Hayes looks very pretty this evening."

Willow cast a cursory glance at Lady Hayes and turned her disbelieving gaze back to Hallie. "Please, even I can lie better than that. You're slipping, Hallie. You used to be better at fibs."

She shrugged, her gaze unnervingly slipping back to Lord Duncannon. As if feeling her inspection, he glanced in her direction, his lips twitching into a rakish grin. Her stomach clenched. Whatever was she going to do about him?

"We're old enough to know that if you were discreet you could take a lover," Willow whispered, leaning in close to ensure privacy. "No one need ever know."

"No," she said, hating the idea. "I've already borne one child out of wedlock, I will not do it again. I'm content as I am. I'm independent, or will be very soon and in the next few months I'll be able to return to Surrey with Ammon and live quietly. I do not need anything to get in the way of that."

"Of course the decision is yours, but you must see that Lord Duncannon may be worth the risk."

"Maybe you ought to take him to your bed since you're so very fond of the idea."

Willow gasped, her eyes widening in shock. "It's not me that he's interested in, otherwise I probably would. I know my aunt wants me to marry well, but after all these years in society and no prospects I fear her dream is in vain. I'm destined to be an old maid. At least I'll have you for company."

Hallie chuckled. "You're incorrigible." She turned back to watch Lord Duncannon. He was deep in conversation with Lord Bankes about something and they both seemed absorbed in the subject matter. Probably horses or dogs.

"Have you kissed him since he's been here? I feel like you're not telling me everything." Willow raised her brow in question.

How could she tell her friend after all that she'd said about his lordship that she had kissed him and some other things. Allowed him to touch her while they were both guests of the baron, to slide up against her body in the most evocative way to tease them both.

She stifled a sigh at the memory of it. It was all deliciousness and a pastime that she could get used to. Even so, there were some things that Willow or any of her friends did not need to know and this was one of them. Nothing would come of their one kiss in the tent and so it would be silly to involve her friend or get her hopes up regarding his lordship.

"No," she lied, taking a sip of her wine. "And nor will it."

~

Robert sipped his whisky and watched Hallie and Lord Duncannon trade heated glances across the room. The silly chit was hot for the man, and he too was a willing participant if he were any judge. Pity his knowledge of Miss Evans would ruin her chances with his lordship. If Lord Duncannon did not turn away from an alliance with this chit when he knew her secrets, then his family would most certainly ensure it occurred.

"Miss Evans," he said, coming to stand beside her. "You're looking particularly pretty this evening. Is that another gown borrowed from Miss Perry?"

Her head whipped about to stare at him and he smiled at the disdain she held in her eyes for him. Good. For he had disdain for her as well.

"It is, Mr. Stewart. How very clever of you to notice. Are you so familiar with the female attire of this house party?"

"Only when it comes to you," he said, taking her arm and leading her away from Willow. Hallie frowned at his gumption. He smirked and continued on.

"I'm glad we're having this moment to better acquaint ourselves. I do love to be informed, to have information about other people. It's a little hobby of mine you could say."

"Really?" she said, her reply bored and uninterested.

"Yes, really, Miss Evans. Shall I tell you a little story that I heard while I was traveling through Rome last year?"

She shrugged, holding her hands at her front. He

glanced at her hands, wondering if that was a little tremor he could see. "Of course, if you wish it."

He chuckled, enjoying this little game more than he thought he would. "That a certain unmarried woman from Felday had borne a child out of wedlock and to an Egyptian general. Can you imagine the scandal? Will you not ask me to whom I may be referring?"

Her skin visibly paled and she refused to look at him. "I will not ask. It seems to be of a private matter," she replied.

Clever girl, but not clever enough. "Well, as to that I can help there," he said, matter-of-fact. "It was you, my dear. Can you imagine such a rumor? However have you survived this long with that tidbit hanging about your neck like a noose?"

She didn't reply and he wondered how long it would be before he claimed any reaction from her. She was a cool one, this Miss Evans, but not cool enough to sneak out of this mess. He wanted her to make a fool of herself. To appear paranoid and unclear with her thinking. She had watched his cousin die without blinking an eye. To make the educated and well-respected Miss Evans pay for her indiscretions was his sole responsibility. His family and their honor demanded it.

"I shall not tease you any longer, Miss Evans. Me knowing your secret must come as a shock, I know, but I will be honest with you as to what I'm going to do with this information, which is more than you ever afforded my cousin. You and your friend did not give his lordship a second chance."

She pulled her arm free of his and stepped back. "Your cousin, sir? I do not understand."

"No you would not, I suppose, but I will explain it to you. Let me just say that I know everything there is to know about you, Miss Evans. I know of Ammon and where he lives. I also know that Omar, your lover, was from a very influential and wealthy family in Cairo. I'm sure they would be very interested in knowing that Omar, their only son, had fathered a boy child."

"You wouldn't dare," she said. He had to give her credit, where he thought she may succumb to the vapors or tears, she instead glared up at him, her mouth pulled into a hard, determined line.

"Oh I would. In fact I have every intention of telling everyone in London and here at this party of who you really are. That you're nothing better than a whore who, although I will credit you with a mind, is still just a woman looking for a hard tup."

"Why are you doing this to me?" she asked and he could almost feel sorry for her. She looked so very pathetic with the fear that lingered in the green depths of her eyes. How sad that as independent a woman Miss Evans was, she'd become pathetic at the first sign of a disagreement.

"My cousin, Lord Oakes probably asked the same thing, before you left him to burn to death. He did not deserve his fate and it was you and Miss Ava Knight who took his future from him. So now I will take your future from you, unless you do as I ask."

She glanced about the room. Robert did the same, noting they were quite alone. "What do you want?" she whispered, her voice trembling.

"Money. I want what you'll earn here at this dig and any other digs into the foreseeable future. I have a future too you see that I need to plan and work toward. You will help me in gaining all that I want."

"But if I give you everything that I earn, what will I

have left to live on? I have expenses just like you, Mr. Stewart."

He shrugged. "Not my concern. You will do as I ask or I'll tell Lord Duncannon and your son's family everything you're hiding and let the dice roll where they will. You may either allow fate to choose your future, or you can. It's up to you."

She stared at him for a moment and he could see her debating, weighing up what he was demanding of her. He watched her with interest, already knowing that she would agree to his demand. What choice did she have? She had no choice.

Miss Evans nodded and walked away, placing down her glass and leaving the room. He smiled. "Just as I thought."

CHAPTER 11

*H*allie fled the drawing room, and seeing people on the staircase and in no mood for idle chat, she headed for the back of the house and the servants' stairs that she used often throughout the day. Tears slipped down her cheeks and she swiped at them, not wanting anyone to see her upset.

What was she going to do? The one hundred and fifty pounds this dig was to be paid to her had been allocated to unpaid debts and stabilizing her and her son's future. She had wanted to purchase some new things for her son and help pay her cousin for his welfare for the past few years. The money was her safety and security when without work. To have to give it away to Mr. Stewart simply because she was involved in his cousin's reign of madness was in itself insanity.

Hallie slumped down on a settee in an unoccupied room, staring at the unlit hearth before her. He would ruin her, that she had no doubt. The hatred she read in his cold eyes was proof of that. To anyone looking at them they would not have seen his hidden loathing of her, but it was there, masked beneath a smiling mouth and charming voice.

Bastard.

She sniffed and dabbed at her face. How was it that men like Mr. Stewart even existed? She doubted he would try such a scheme with a gentleman. No, he only targeted women. Women like her who had a lot to lose and who had no family, no brother to defend them.

"Hallie?"

She jumped and turned to see Lord Duncannon standing at the door, the light from the hall behind him illuminating him but leaving his features too dark to read.

"Can I help you, my lord?" she asked, turning to look back at the hearth, not wanting him to see her upset.

"I saw you with Mr. Stewart and you appeared upset by his conversation. I wanted to ensure he has not injured you in any way."

She shut her eyes in part exasperation that Lord Duncannon was aware of her enough to know when she was injured and part pleasure that he cared enough to see if she were well. "Mr. Stewart was simply being a man. No need to worry about me, my lord. I'm perfectly capable of looking after myself." She sighed. Of course by paying Mr. Stewart her salary, she would keep his mouth closed for some months, or at least until she found further employment and then his threats would start again. How long did he plan on keeping this threat over her head?

Forever, probably. Who would not keep asking for funds and therefore not have to work themselves? A great many people she would imagine.

Lord Duncannon came into the room, shutting the

door behind him before sitting beside her. She hoped that he could not see that she'd been crying or he would know she had lied and he could then possibly make a scene with Mr. Stewart when not knowing all the facts. There was no knowing what the man was capable of if threatened. He would more than likely shout out to all who were present that she had slept with an Egyptian general and had his child out of wedlock.

"You're upset," he said, taking her hand and pulling her toward him.

How had he known? The man must have night vision to have seen that she'd been crying. His presence overwhelmed her, tempting her to lean into his warmth and care. To stay there forever.

"Nothing of concern, my lord. Please do not pry," she said, hoping he would let the subject drop.

"Hallie," he pleaded, reaching up and clasping her jaw, turning her to face him. "You would tell me if something was wrong. You know that I would help you with anything. I do not like to see you distressed."

She pulled her jaw free of his hand. His touch made her want things that she should not. Things that in the past now placed her in the predicament she now faced. The man was trouble, but in a completely different manner to what trouble Mr. Stewart brought her. One night in his arms was starting to be very difficult to deny herself, especially when to escape into that dream could remove her from the nightmare that Mr. Stewart made her live in.

"I'm tired, that is all, my lord. I think I shall retire for the night." She went to stand and he stayed her by touching her arm.

"Must you go? I've not seen you today. Lord Bankes

asked me to ride out with him to his tenant farms and view some of his land. I could not refuse."

"There are more eligible and suitable women in the drawing room, Lord Duncannon. It confuses me still as to why you would waste your time with me. We do not suit." The memory of Arthur in her bed that night in Surrey bombarded her mind. She supposed that they did not suit was not entirely true. They did suit very well when thrown together in such circumstances. But the idea of forever, well, that was an absurdity that she could not let herself believe in.

His touch the other day at the dig site, the scorching heat and need he made her body feel even now tempted her. Tempted her when it shouldn't. Long after he'd returned to working in the trench, she had burned for his touch, to feel his unrelenting lips against her own. She was doomed if such wants continued. A fault within her that she wanted things similar to men. Wanting the same freedom, but unable to have it.

"I do not care what anyone thinks. I need you to know and believe that you are the woman that I crave. The one and only woman that I want in my bed." He shuffled closer still, clasping her face with both hands. "I burn for you, Hallie. I have for years. I know our history is as turbulent as that first carriage ride you offered me in Surrey, but you are the only woman that I've never been able to forget. I do not want to regret not knowing if you and I can be more than our history."

She stared at him, her mind tumbling to understand what he was saying. "I'm not for you, Arthur. Your family would never accept me, and if you knew me at all, I know that you would not either." Hallie reached up and clasped his hands, pulling them down to sit in her lap. "I would be lying if I did not admit to wanting you. That at night the longing in me to be with you makes me want to throw all rules of etiquette aside and sneak into your room, but it would not change anything. There are things in my past that I cannot change and they are things that I do not believe you or your family would understand. Please know that I cannot give you what you want. I risk too much by such actions."

He frowned, his hands clasping hers in a relentless grip. "What has happened that makes you believe that? I know my family, once they meet you, they will adore you. You are a gentleman's daughter and I am a gentleman. I see no reason why I cannot court you at least."

Her breath hitched at the sweetness of him. To be courted and flirted with sounded heavenly, if she were not a woman who had taken a lover out of wedlock and birthed his child with no regrets.

"I'm past being courted. That time has long expired."

"Please," he begged, squeezing her hands. "Let me at least try to win you and if you do not wish to pursue a future with me, then I shall leave you alone. I promise you that."

Hallie stood and walked over to the window, looking out at the dark grounds that had only the smallest amount of moonlight to light anyone's way. She thought over his proposition. Not that she thought it could lead to anything, but then if Mr. Stewart thought she were being pursued by Lord Duncannon he may also leave her alone. He may, in fact, stop his threats.

She turned to his lordship, hating in part that she was using him to keep Mr. Stewart at arm's length. "Very well. I shall let you court me, but please know that I do not believe that anything can come of this union. Even so, it'll be nice to be flirted with by a handsome gentleman."

He grinned and stood, coming over to her. "You think I'm handsome."

She chuckled. "You know you are," she said, sucking in a breath as he stepped close to her person, his chest brushing hers and making her body ache.

"You're so beautiful." His breath tickled across her lips.

Hallie could get used to Arthur speaking to her in such a way. It had been a long time since she'd had such sweet words whispered to her. Even with everything working against them, his family and her past, still she could not help but fall into the dance of courtship.

She leaned into him and kissed him, inwardly smiled as he stilled a moment in surprise before hoisting her up hard against him and kissing her back. His lips took hers, and she opened for him immediately, wanting to feel his touch, the slide of his tongue against hers, his heat and desire. All of it just for her.

Being with him was delicious.

Their kiss, just like all that they'd shared went from sweet and tempting to hot and demanding within a moment. Only with Arthur did she ever have this reaction. This need that rose within her and left her aching and wanting more. Always more.

"We should stop. Anyone could walk in," she gasped, pulling away. He kissed down her neck, his tongue sliding against her collar bone. She clutched at his shoulders, her knees weak all of a sudden.

"God, you smell good." He kissed up to her ear, licking her lobe. Hallie shut her eyes, a shiver raking her body. Blast it, he was good at seduction. Good at making whatever woman was in his arms feel special. "It's hard to stop," he admitted.

With great difficulty, she pushed at his chest, separating them. He stepped back, disappointment written across his face. A disappointment she could well understand as she too was feeling it right at this moment.

"Are you heading up to the dig site tomorrow?"

"Yes," she said, checking her gown and making sure her hair was just as it was before they started clutching at each other. "Will you be coming up to help me? I'm hoping to start a second trench tomorrow."

He came up behind her, wrapping his arms about her waist and kissing her neck quickly. "I will be. I have some missives to write to my steward first, and then I'll be up there. I'll bring lunch if you wish to picnic with me."

The idea of having a lovely repast with him at the dig site, a place that she found pleasure just being near, nevertheless working at, made her heart beat fast. That Arthur not only liked what she did but supported her, told her that perhaps he was no longer the rogue he was reputed to be. Not all men would be so accommodating. Certainly not titled ones.

"I would like that. Thank you."

❧

*A*rthur spent the morning writing letters to his steward regarding his two estates and then set about writing a letter to his grandmother. He'd been putting off sending her a missive simply because the last time that she had written him, she had gone on, to no end, regarding his continued bachelorhood and his lack of prospects or inclination toward marriage.

That had all changed. The kiss the other day at the dig site for starters, and now just last night had seemed to be a turning point with him and Hallie. That she was allowing him to court her was a big step for her, and a massive relief for him.

Now he had to write to his grandmother and explain what he was about and who he was courting. He was certain that once she met Hallie she would fall in love with her as much as he feared he was well on the way to doing.

He'd never felt such a connection with anyone before in his life and to finally have her back in England and willing to see what may come of them was a desire he'd never thought would come to fruition.

"Ah, Lord Duncannon, may I come in? There is a book on botany that Baron Bankes mentioned and I'm most eager to look through it."

Arthur glanced up from signing the letter to his grandmother and nodded to Mr. Stewart, who stood at the threshold of the room. "Of course. Please, come in. I'm almost finished here in any case."

The gentleman scanned the bookshelves as Arthur wax-sealed his missives and stamped them with his family emblem. Out the corner of his eye he watched the man's progress, something about the gentleman not sitting right with him. Arthur could not exactly say what it was about him that he distrusted, maybe a gut instinct, but there was something decidedly off about the man. Hallie certainly did not like him, and his presence discomfited her, more than she would admit. He would bear keeping an eye on.

"What a delightful house party," Mr. Stewart said, his back to Arthur as he continued his search. "I do not think I've ever been to one with such congenial guests. Do you not agree, Lord Duncannon?"

Arthur had been to many house parties over the years, some with much more friendly and agreeable persons, but then Mr. Stewart may not have been to as many as he and so he nodded, showing his support. "It has been a most pleasant stay."

"Have you been up to the archaeological dig site yet? I must admit that I'm yet to look in on it, but I do believe the woman who's in charge of it, Miss Evans, is most accomplished."

"She is," he agreed, at least on this point Mr. Stewart was indeed quite correct. "They are starting a new trench tomorrow in fact. I'm sure in the days to come they will find many new artifacts to date and explain."

"Oh yes, no doubt," Mr. Stewart readily agreed. "I understand she spent some time in Egypt. How very exotic of her. The stories she could tell if only she would." He chuckled. "Do you not agree, my lord?"

Arthur set the letters on the silver slaver on the desk for the staff to post and leaned back in the leather wing-back chair. He steepled his fingers before him, watching Mr. Stewart stroll about the shelves. He narrowed his eyes, starting to doubt his sole purpose here was to discuss Hallie and not this book on botany at all.

The pit of his gut clenched at the idea that Mr. Stewart may like Hallie more than he was letting on and was looking to see if he had any competition. "I should imagine she would know a great deal about the area and the people. I know through mutual friends she was very much in love with the country."

"Maybe there is more to that than we know," he said. "Women, after all, are mysterious beings with many thoughts and dreams inside their minds."

Arthur stared at Mr. Stewart's back, the idea that

Hallie had more of a life than work in Egypt had never entered his mind. He didn't think the culture allowed for balls like those he'd attended at Almacks with his numerous friends. That did not mean that they did not occur or that she'd had the ability to meet people. Men…

"Ah ha, here it is," he said, holding up the thick tome and showing Arthur. "I'm so glad Baron Bankes had not led me on a merry chase. A book such as this is just what I need in such a large and lonely estate."

Arthur stared down at the desk, thinking of Hallie and her time abroad. "I hope you enjoy your book," he said, standing. "Do visit the dig site, Mr. Stewart. I think you'll find it quite interesting."

The man did not reply, merely nodded. Arthur strode out into the entrance and started for his room. What Mr. Stewart had said gave Arthur pause. He'd never thought about Hallie in Egypt and her many years there must have been taken up with more than just archaeological digs. Of course their days were long and arduous and very much hard work, but that did not mean that was the only thing Hallie did when away.

Had someone abroad courted her? There were many Englishmen who traveled abroad, who went to Egypt and farther east to survey and learn of new lands. Had any one of them shown an interest in Hallie? Why else would Mr. Stewart say such a thing? The man was not to be trusted and Arthur could not help but think that he was hinting at something.

But what?

He rubbed his jaw, thinking over the prospect. It did not mean that Hallie had been courted by an Englishman at all. What if there had been a man from Egypt who had captured her attention? Had courted her?

And loved her as much as he was fearing he was starting to.

~

*H*allie threw herself into work over the next few days. The new trench was well underway, a slow process by hand and she couldn't help but hope that one day such tasks could be made easier with some invention or contraption of some type.

Unfortunately Mr. Stewart had paid her a visit only yesterday, spouting on about what they had found and how very interesting it was to discover things that were lost. One of his particular comments about the past and how things never stayed buried for long was of particular interest and seemed to make him laugh at his own threats.

She had looked at him, wanting him to see how much she loathed him and his blackmailing. She could not trust him or that he would keep his mouth shut if she paid him. He was up to something other than taking her hard-earned money, and the pit of her stomach churned that he would not be satisfied with that compensation.

After an hour or so she had been glad to see him go and she was most especially pleased with the shower of rain that had passed through that had ensured his departure. For all of his spouting off of enjoying her type of work and being outdoors in nature, he didn't have a very fine opinion of the location or weather.

The rain unfortunately had continued to pass through Somerset and she had to abandon the dig site, heading back to the estate several hours earlier than planned. The men had laid tarps over the trenches to try to stop the soil from bogging up too much, but as the afternoon ticked away, the rain only seemed to get heavier.

Hallie ordered a bath, and with the help of a maid was able to remove her soaked clothing with little trouble.

"I shall take it downstairs to dry, Miss Evans. Will you be needing anything else before I go?"

"No, thank you," she said, walking to the door to lock it before she bathed. "I'll not be needing anything else tonight." Hallie locked the door and then thankfully alone, sank down in her hot bath. The servants had placed it before the well-lit fire and she lay back, relaxing in the little luxury this house stay afforded.

She smiled at the thought of being back at her cottage in Felday. The small house didn't have room for such a big bath. They would have to make do with a hip bath and one in the kitchen when the need arose.

Hallie picked up the soap that smelled of fresh herbs and cleaned the day's grime from her skin. Once this job was completed, she had hoped to do one or two more archaeological digs before collecting her son from her cousin and returning to Surrey. Mr. Stewart's threat now stopped her from following her plan.

Whatever was she going to do?

Maybe she could seek the gentleman out and ask him to rethink his threat. There were very few she could turn to. Of course Willow would help her, but then if society found out about her child and that she was unmarried, people associated with her would be tainted.

She could not tell Willow of Mr. Stewart's demand, for she knew her friend would defend her even if it were at her own peril.

Sadly the idea of burying Mr. Stewart in one of her trenches had come to mind. It would certainly fix all her problems and for a man to threaten a vulnerable woman, she doubted he'd be missed very much in this world.

A light knock sounded on her door and she sat up in the bath, the water splashing over the side. "Who is it?" she asked, thankful she'd locked the door.

"It's me. Duncannon. I need to speak to you."

She sat in the bath a moment longer, unsure if she wanted to speak to him. Every time she was around him, he made her feel and do things that she'd promised herself never to feel or do since losing Omar. Even so, she stood, clasping the towel off a nearby chair and wrapped it about herself, walking to the door. "What do you want?" she whispered, hoping no one saw his lordship whispering at her door like a lover after a midnight tryst.

"Can you meet me in the downstairs back parlor? Everyone is in the front drawing room waiting for dinner to be announced, but I need to speak to you."

Hallie frowned. What did Lord Duncannon need to speak to her about? "I'll be down directly. I'll meet you there."

She listened at the door as his receding footsteps sounded on the carpeted passageway. Hallie dressed quickly in a clean afternoon gown. The bodice was a little snug and the cut of the dress was a couple of years old, but it was still reasonably unworn and suited her coloring.

As she made her way downstairs, she couldn't help but wonder what he wanted to discuss. She also couldn't help but debate whether she should confide in him about Mr. Stewart. She didn't have to mention her son, but she could mention what her past in Egypt had been, and that Mr. Stewart was threatening to expose. It would give her a good indication of what Lord Duncannon thought of her actions.

Her past as a woman who had fallen in love and slept with another man out of wedlock. If he was supportive and not offensive toward her, he may be someone she could turn to for help, to eventually tell of her boy. Lord Duncannon had powerful friends, many of whom could make Mr. Stewart keep his mouth closed and leave her alone for good.

The drawing room was dark, and yet a small candle burned on the mantel and the fire had been lit. Lord Duncannon came over to her as she entered and locked the door behind her, helping her to a chair before the hearth.

"There is something that I need to ask you and you may tell me to go to the devil, but I really do hope you're able to give me the truth."

"If I can I will." She looked up at him as he sat on a nearby chair, working his hands in his lap. Nerves pooled in her stomach that perhaps Mr. Stewart had already been at work with his lordship and poisoning his mind against her.

"I'm nervous to ask you what I want," he admitted.

Hallie smiled to put him at ease and yet her stomach churned. What was it he wanted to know? Or worse, what did he suspect? "Ask me, Arthur, or you'll make me as nervous as you are."

He took a deep breath, meeting her with a steady gaze. "I wanted to ask you about your time in Egypt. What your life was like there."

Everything within her stilled. To ask such a question made it abundantly clear that Mr. Stewart had been whispering ideas into people's heads. Who else had he spoken to? What other suggestions had he made them think? Of course, she could be turning paranoid, but she highly doubted it. The man was bent on ruining her reputation. "It was a very busy life. We had multiple dig sites that Mr. Shelly was overseeing and every day a new artifact was found and catalogued. You're the benefactor of the British Museum, surely you would know as well as anyone how busy we were. The museum did take delivery of multiple artifacts from us."

"Of course," he said, a small frown between his eyes. She watched him a moment and could see he was struggling with some truth or a question that he wasn't certain he should ask. Or know how to breach. "Did you have much of a social life in Egypt?"

And there it was, the one question that she had been dreading. Even so, a little relief poured through her that he'd asked. She didn't have to tell him about Ammon, but she would not hide the courtship with Omar. She had loved him, with all her heart and no one would ever change that wonderful time in her life. "I enjoyed dinners and balls similar to those held in London at the Consul General's home in Cairo. Mr. Henry Salt had close ties with the ruler of Egypt, the Pasha Mohamed Ali, and the evenings were always interesting and pleasurable. Mr. Salt is an Egyptologist, and immensely clever. You know him of course."

"I have met him once or twice. He has given antiquities to the British Museum as well."

"Of course," she said, well believing that. "Just as in England, the ruler of Egypt had a militia, men who were under his rule and protected him. They too were often at these events, but always watching, not taking too much of an interest." Except for one of course. Omar, who had seen Hallie from across the room, and her world had stopped at the sight of him. His too, she knew.

Lord Duncannon's eyes narrowed on her and she could see he was weighing her words. "Did you…" He cleared his throat. "Were you courted while abroad?"

Hallie raised her brows as she thought back on that time. How the sight of Omar had made her heart skip a beat. He had not moved, merely watched, and yet his eyes had heated with interest at the sight of her and she had known, somehow, in some way, their lives would intertwine.

"My time in Egypt was very memorable and pleasant. I shall miss it forever."

He watched her and she could see in his eyes that he wanted no secrets between them. If he was serious about courting her she supposed they shouldn't have secrets, but something in Arthur's eyes gave her pause. A fear of hearing of her past may cause him to not like what he heard stilled her tongue. Stopped her from forming the words that she'd fallen in love in that wonderous, ancient land and regretted not a bit of it.

"I want us to be honest with each other, Hallie. No secrets."

"There is nothing that you need to know, my lord," she lied, hoping he could not read her too well or tell when she was trying to hide a secret. He was not ready to hear her truths, and in all honestly, she was not ready to tell him. Not really.

"What about you?" she asked, changing the subject matter. "You're well known in London and many mama's wish to turn your head toward their charges. Is there no one that your grandmother has chosen for you?"

He chuckled, leaning back in his chair, steepling his fingers. "I'm sure there are many, but none of them would suit. I've never been one for meek and mild," he said, giving her a pointed look that made her skin warm.

She wasn't fool enough not to know he meant her. He wanted to court her after all, but still, there were so many secrets between them. So many things that he'd dislike if only he knew the truth. For a moment she debated telling him everything anyway, laying her whole life in Egypt on the table, and letting the axe fall on her neck or not.

Lord Duncannon she was certain was above all a man of honor, but then, some were thin-skinned when it came to women and thinking they'd been duped by the fairer sex.

"I suppose that explains why you're courting me then. I'm neither of those things."

"No you're not." He came and sat beside her. His nearness overwhelmed her. Terrible as it was, scandalous even, she longed to be held, to be the whole focus of someone else. The way Lord Duncannon made her feel was reminiscent of how she'd felt with Omar and it was heady indeed.

He reached up, tracing her lips with his finger. "You're so beautiful you make my breath catch every time I see you."

Nerves fluttered in her stomach. "Even when I'm dressed in my breeches and covered in mud?" she teased, trying to lighten the mood. His steely gaze put paid to that attempt of denial and she swallowed.

"Even then."

She gasped as he took her lips in a fierce kiss, his tongue sweeping across hers. Her head spun a moment before she wrapped her arms about his neck and kissed him back. She'd wanted to kiss him again too. Every time she'd caught a glimpse of him on the grounds, strong and tall, muscular and lean, her hands itched to run across his body. To feel his warm skin against hers, his touch on her person.

"You drive me to distraction," he admitted, kissing her deeper still.

She pulled back, meeting his gaze. "It's the same for me too," she said, kissing him again and losing herself to him and to all he offered, for now at least.

CHAPTER 12

*A*rthur tried to rein in his need for Hallie, but her sweet gasps and her decadent kisses made his wits spiral. He clasped her face and took all that she was willing to give him. He'd longed for this woman in his arms from the very moment they had been parted. He'd dreamed about her constantly and with the few women he'd bedded over the years, all of them paled in comparison to her.

He did not care what his family thought of his choice, it was well and truly made. A wife without wits, a society doll that pandered to the *ton*, gossiped and took tea all day long made his jaw ache in distaste.

He found himself lowering her on the settee, coming over her. Hallie would never bore him, her mind alone was sharp enough to keep him on his toes. She loved travel and would be willing to visit foreign places without hesitation. Their life appeared before him, rich and full and he couldn't grasp it soon enough.

She was all soft curves and womanly flesh that made him ache. He settled atop her, basking in her warmth and acquiescence. He wanted this life with a desperation that scared him, and yet he could not help but feel she was hiding something from him. Her hesitation in answering him regarding her time in Egypt was telling.

Maybe Mr. Stewart was hinting at something after all. Was it so bad that she could not confide in him? He would never do anything that hurt her, he'd paid for that mistake for seven years, he wouldn't do it again.

One of her legs slipped about his and she pressed herself against him. He rubbed his hard-as-rock cock against her mons and she moaned through their kiss. Just as she was in life, in the private setting they were now in she was reactive, thrilling, and as sweet as he remembered.

It would be so easy to seduce her, but he would not. Not here. He needed her to trust him above anything else, and to see what they could be together. He would not rush her in this.

He pulled back, his breathing ragged and, looking down at her, he noticed her breath too was labored, her breasts straining against her bodice. The scent of flowers rose from her skin and he knew she'd bathed before coming downstairs. The image of her being in a bath, lathing soap and relaxing in water made him groan.

"I should escort you back to your room before anything further progresses tonight. We're in no rush."

She bit her lip, her eyes wide and a little cloudy with arousal. Her gaze dipped to his lips and he inwardly swore. Her thoughts stating otherwise as clear as the written word. The choice was impossible. He didn't want to leave. He wanted to hoist up her gown, slide down low on the settee and feast on her, every part of her person. Then, and only when he had her writhing in pleasure, and begging for him to take her, would he sheathe himself into her welcoming heat.

He shut his eyes, trying to blot out the image of doing exactly that.

"You should." She slipped her other leg about his, pulling him hard up against her core. Unable to stop himself, he slid against her flesh, the pleasure rocking him to his center. His body roared to have her.

She lifted her hips, grinding against him, taking her own pleasure when he didn't move.

"Damn it, Hallie. Stop."

A wicked grin slipped across her lips and his control snapped. He thrust against her, and she gasped into their kiss. The delicious friction was too much. He would not come here. Not in a drawing room at Baron Bankes's house party.

This time he found the strength to tear himself away and he stood, walking over to the window and hoisting it up. The cool, night air went someway in chilling his skin and cooling his need for her. He leaned over the sill, his brain demanding that he turn and finish what they both wanted.

And damn it all to hell he wanted her.

He felt her come up behind him and he straightened. She wrapped her hands about his waist from behind, holding him tight. "You make it hard to stop. I will tell you a secret and then you can walk me to my room."

Her hands slipped over his chest and his breath caught when her fingers dipped between the buttons on his waist-coat and slipped against his shirt.

"What is it?" he asked, curious and wanting to know everything there was to know about her. His grandmother would say he was a little obsessed with her, and perhaps he was, but his certainty that she was the one for him had never waned. Not even after all the years they were apart had it lessened.

"Even with all my plans to travel abroad that I had before meeting you in Felday, there was a small part of me that hoped you'd return that morning. That fate had placed you before me and that I should listen to its call. I think we both missed an opportunity that day, one that I'm unsure we can ever get back."

He turned, frowning down at her. "We can get it back, Hallie. The feelings that I had for you then have done nothing but doubled since that day. I will earn your affection and trust. I promise I'll never hurt you again."

She nodded, and he could see that her eyes had gone a little glassy with emotion. "I will hold you to that promise, Lord Duncannon."

"I hope you do, Miss Evans." *Always.*

~

*H*allie woke to the sound of heavy rain hitting the windowpane. She pushed back the covers on her bed and walked to the window, pulling back the dark, velvet drapes to see bad weather had settled in and didn't look to be going anywhere.

She sighed, debating what she should do. There was much work to do up at the dig site and she could still accomplish that in the small tent that had been erected for her workshop.

Finishing her morning toilette, she dressed in breeches, shirt, and jacket, and slipped on her greatcoat and broad-brimmed hat that she had used in Egypt. It would serve to keep the rain from dripping down her neck just as it stopped the sun from burning her skin.

The walk up the excavation site took longer than normal. The ground was already wet and boggy, her boots sinking half an inch with each step. The site was vacant of any workers and that suited her fine. She went into the tent, happy to see everything was where she'd left it last. Hallie lit a lamp and got out her sketchbook, needing to sketch their finds of the day before and explain what she believed they were.

For some hours she worked, drawing and studying while outside the rain relentlessly hit the canvas roof, lulling her with its calming rhythm.

The canvas flap of the tent flipped open and she jumped at the sight of Lord Duncannon, a warm swirl of pleasure blossoming inside her at the sight of him.

He sighed, the sound tinged with relief. "You're here," he said, more to himself as he stepped into the tent, shuffling out of his greatcoat. He ran a hand through his wet, dripping hair, leaving the golden strands on end. He looked deadly handsome and after last night she wasn't sure it was a good idea that they were alone together. He had left her unfulfilled, and all night she'd tossed and turned, wanting more.

To be teased in such a way without gaining release was not what she constituted as a gentlemanly thing to do.

"I am. I'm cataloguing our finds. What are you doing here? You're soaked through." She took in his clothing, his damp breeches and shirt that clung to his person and accentuated his every delicious curve of muscle on his abdomen. Hallie was unable to tear her eyes from his chest.

"You should probably stop looking at me as if you'd like to take a bite out of me before I let you," he teased, sending her a wicked grin. "I had not seen you about the house and I grew concerned. When your maid said that you had left before she had time to serve you breakfast, I came to check on you."

She chuckled. "Did you think I had run away, my lord? That your seduction last evening had scared me?"

He didn't say anything for a moment, simply stared at her a little mute before he cleared his throat, once again pushing back his hair. The action did little to cool her ardour. If she were honest with herself, she had started to think that she was a little preoccupied with him. More than was healthy. For both of them.

"It worried me that it had."

She looked at him quickly. "Why?"

He raised his brow, walking about her work table, picking up a few of her finds, inspecting them before placing them back down. "The thought of being with you again is what gets me up each morning and keeps me moving forward throughout the day. That the idea of not having you in sight, of having you by my side as we walk through this life scares me. That what I feel for you is stronger than what I've felt for anyone ever and that you may not reciprocate that emotion."

Hallie stilled at his words, having not expected such honesty from his lordship. Nor did she think that what he'd said would resonate so much within her. Last evening she'd wanted to keep walking along the corridor to his room, shut the doors on the world and become lost in each other's arms.

The stab of disappointment when he'd done exactly what he said he would had been profound. Even now, here up at the dig site, all she could think about was being with him like that again, and possibly more.

Her gaze flicked to the makeshift trundle bed that had

been brought up for her, just in case she was caught here or in need of rest. Now it glowed like a beacon of pleasure. They were, no one would venture up here today with the bad, relentless weather.

Nerves pitted in her stomach and she busied her hand on her sketch of the small, round coin she had found.

"You have beautiful hands. Do you know that?" His hand that had been sliding across the wooden table top, slipped across the top of hers and slowly made its way up her arm. A shiver ran down her spine and she looked up, meeting his gaze. It was heavy with desire and she took a calming breath, placing down her pencil.

"You're touching my arm, my lord."

His teasing gleam entered his eyes. "I am."

She stood, her eyes level with his neck, his very nice neck that led to an even nicer abdomen that even now, years after she'd seen it last, still made her hands itch to touch. Hallie was sick of denying herself. It was obvious that he wanted her just as much as she wanted him. His breathing was deep and although slow, she knew to her very core he was trying to rein in his desire.

She didn't want him to.

Leaning forward she kissed the little dip at the middle of his throat, working her way along his shoulder blade. He sucked in a breath and she gasped as he leaned down, clasping her face and bringing her up to meet his kiss. It was deep and a little wild and sparked her desire.

She wrapped her arms about his neck and he lifted her off her feet, placing her on the wooden table, taking care not to ruin any of her work. He stood back, ripping at his cravat, never once losing eye contact with her. Hallie bit her lip as he threw off his coat and waistcoat before tugging his shirt free from his breeches and pulling it over his head.

He was simply beautiful, as perfect as she remembered him. All defined muscles and lines, his stomach taut and flexing with each breath. She ran her hand over him, marveling at his beauty. Heat pooled at her core and she ached to have him.

"Now it's your turn." He reached out and one by one, undid the small buttons that ran down the front of her shirt. Just like him she had breeches on, preferring to wear them instead of dresses when working at dig sites. He slid her shirt free from her breeches and glided it over her shoulders, letting it lay on the table.

His hand cupped her breast through her stays and she shut her eyes, reveling in the contact that she'd been starved of for so long.

"So perfect," he whispered, slipping her stays down her chest and exposing her to his view. She had not been so exposed to a man in years and the urge to cover herself was strong, but she forced her hands upon the table, letting him take his fill of her. Arthur leaned forward and kissed her breast, placing soft, sweet kisses against her nipple. His tongue slipped over her pebbled flesh and she cupped his head, holding him against her.

"I missed this. All of you." He made short work of the laces and, throwing them to the floor with little care, bared her to his view. Arthur grabbed her breeches at the front and pulled her off the table to stand. "Now these have to go."

Hallie reached down, slipping the buttons free at the fall and sliding them down her legs. She kicked them to the side before meeting Arthur's heated gaze that threatened to melt her into a liquid mess. She was as naked as a babe and yet, the pleasure on his face, the reverence that she read there, pushed away any doubt or fear.

Without help, she sat on the table, leaning back on her hands, waiting for him. "Are you going to join me here, my lord?"

He swallowed, the sound almost audible. "Arthur. Please, call me Arthur."

She grinned. "Will you join me here…Arthur?"

~

Oh hell yes he would.

He'd go to hell and back if only he could live the rest of his life with the woman before him. How had he let her go all those years ago? He should have told his friends to damn well stop the carriage and let him out. He should have forced her to take him with her to Egypt and never leave her side. Should have was a tormenting beast he loathed. So many mistakes that he could not take back.

Need riding him hard, he ripped at his frontfalls and pushed his breeches down and off. He stepped between her legs and a feeling of rightness swamped him. His cock strained between them, and he fought not to rush. To take his time and savor this moment. She wrapped her arms about his shoulders and he kissed her, tasting tea and honey on her sweet lips.

Reaching down he clasped one of her thighs, taking his time enjoying her warm, soft flesh, slipping his cock against her wet, willing cunny.

She moaned against his mouth and he nipped her lip. "You like that," he said, sliding against her heat again and gaining a moan of approval.

"Oh yes."

Her hand traced down his shoulder, down to his waist, before circling his member. Her hand slid down his phallus, teasing him with long, constant strokes and for a moment Arthur thought he saw stars.

He shut his eyes, enjoying the friction her touch brought forth. His balls tightened and he reached down, stilling her hand. "You'll make me lose myself."

Watching, she guided him into her wet heat. She engulfed him, warm and tight. His body roared to take her, hard and fast, fuck her until they were both spent and gasping for breath.

God fucking damn it, she felt good.

Her mouth opened on a sigh and he kissed her, pulling her hard against him, their flesh touching from breast to legs. He thrust into her, and realized it would never be enough. He needed her more than ever before. She wrapped her leg about his hip, holding him against her with her foot. He fucked her, hard and fast. Heedless of where they were or the fact that anyone could come into the tent at any moment.

She was his, of this he was certain and she would be his wife if he could convince her to take him as her husband.

Arthur increased his pace, the feel of her willing body, her little gasps and sighs drove him senseless. He pulled back from kissing her, watching her as he took her. Her lips swollen and a little red from his kisses, her eyes cloudy with desire.

"Yes," she gasped, watching him, her hands tight on his shoulders as he thrust relentlessly into her heat. She threw her head back, her hair spilling down her spine. He leaned forward, kissing her neck in harsh little pecks. "Just like that. Don't stop," she gasped, her white, straight teeth biting her bottom lip.

Arthur did as she asked, dared not to do anything that would not bring her pleasure.

A mewling sound and his name spewed from her lips. He gritted his teeth, needing her to shatter about him before he'd take his pleasure. Sweat beaded off their skin, no matter the cool day. And then he felt the strong, pulling shudders around his cock, dragging him along to the road of pleasure. He wrenched free at the last moment, spilling onto the dirt floor beneath the table, his hand working his cock as he watched as Hallie caught her breath and composure.

She sat up, leaning once again on her arms, one leg swinging idly over the table. A satisfied smile played about her lips. "It should rain more often if that's how I'm to pass the time here when you visit."

He chuckled, stepping between her legs and pulling her close. "You do realize there will be no getting rid of me now."

She shrugged one perfect shoulder. "You're not so bad."

He clasped her face. "Neither are you," he said, kissing her again and losing himself once more in her arms.

CHAPTER 13

$\mathcal{T}$he rain unfortunately stopped overnight. The ground up at the dig site was still waterlogged and so Hallie continued cataloguing her finds and sketching them, making a journal and map of everything they had found and where on the map she'd sketched before digging up the trenches.

Once again she was alone on the dig site, and yet, when she was packing up her pencils and sketchbook it was not Arthur who met her outside to walk her back to the estate, but Mr. Stewart.

She greeted him with cool civility, having hoped she'd not be caught alone with him again. He was trouble, mostly trouble for her and she was still uncertain how she would survive if he wanted all her money that she earned.

"How is progress coming along, Miss Evans?"

"Very well, thank you," she said, buttoning up her greatcoat and slipping on her broadbrimmed hat and starting back down the hill toward the estate. She had left later than anticipated and in the distance she could see the lights at Baron Bankes's estate were already alight and shining through the many windows in preparation for the evening festivities.

"I thought while we had a minute to ourselves we should discuss if you've had any further enquiries about similar digs you may be interested in. You remember our deal of course or do you need reminding?"

She rounded on him, glaring up at the popinjay. He was a leach that society would expel, any level of society for anyone within half a mile of this man would know he was not good. Rotten to the core like fruit with a worm in it. "You would ruin my life, take everything from me simply because you cannot accept the fact that your cousin was a madman who killed people and almost killed my friend. How dare you, sir."

He grabbed her arm, squeezing her hard. She fought not to flinch under his assault. "I would dare, yes. My cousin was innocent and it was only because your friend fucked a duke that she wasn't caught out for the scheming, lying bitch that she is. My cousin wrote to me, I knew his character better than anyone. The things they accused him of were ludicrous. He would never do any of those things."

"Neither would my friend," she spat back at him, wrenching out of his hold. "And if you touch me again, I'll bloody your nose. Do you understand that, Mr. Stewart?"

He laughed, the sound condescending and repellent. "You owe me a debt that will be paid and will continue to be paid until I deem it appropriate for you to stop. Until then, remember I know all about your life in Egypt and the dirty little secret you have. Whatever will Lord Duncannon think when he finds out the woman he's cock happy for fucked another when abroad? Tell me, Miss Evans," he said, rubbing his jaw with his hand. "Have you always been free with your wiles?"

Without thought, she struck him across the face. The crack of the slap ricocheted up her arm and she fisted her hand as pain spiked through her palm.

"I will give you that one, my dear, but you'll only get one. The next time you hit me, I'll hit back."

Hallie stood still and watched as he continued down the hill toward the house as if he had not a care in the world. *Bastard.* Tears burned her eyes and her vision of the woods swam before her. Whatever would she do? Could she tell Lord Duncannon?

Fear that what Mr. Stewart accused her of put paid to that idea. His lordship would think her fast if she told him the truth. As for her son, that would be the final straw and he would never think of her again knowing she had a child.

His family would be right in keeping him away from her. She wasn't pure, not from a great, well-to-do family, nor had she ever wanted to be. He would soon come to realize that his foolish dreams of them were unrealistic.

Not that she cared as to what his family thought of her, but she wouldn't put her son in a situation where he would be looked down upon, disregarded and treated unfairly. Not by Arthur and certainly not by his grandmother who was a formidable force in the *ton.*

Love had its limits, love for others at least. Her son and her love for him was not a price she was willing to pay to have the man she had started to think of more than she should. To see a life that they could have and dream. If only there weren't so many other factors that would tear them apart she would try for a life with him.

But she wasn't fool enough to follow that thought. Their affection was doomed and so too was their time.

~

*A*rthur found Hallie in the library the following day. She was seated on the floor behind a group of shelving. Baron Bankes had a well-stocked library that looked more like a book store with its many shelves lined up in a row at one end of the room. His lordship had taken most of the houseguests out for a walk down to the river that ran through his estate, but Arthur had remained scarce until they had left.

He watched her chew her bottom lip as she leaned over an old tome, her hair hastily tied back in a single ribbon, strands of her dark hair slipping over her face. An ache formed in his chest and he cleared his throat, making his presence known.

She glanced up at him and he had hoped to see pleasure on her features. Instead, all he saw was trepidation and regret. Unease slithered down his spine and he sat, stretching his legs out before him and crossing his feet.

"Lord Duncannon, please join me," she said, her tone oozing with sarcasm.

He glanced at her, meeting her eyes. "I had hoped we were past formal titles, Miss Evans. You were Hallie to me yesterday and I was Arthur. Can we not be that again?"

"What you ask is impossible," she said, closing the tome hard, eliciting a puff of dust.

He waved the dust away, coughing. "Nothing is impossible. Your travels abroad and the work that you did there is proof of that." She glared at the bookcase before her, not looking at him. Whatever was wrong? He mentally retraced everything that had passed between them since yesterday, and they had parted on good terms. Very good in fact.

She sighed, turning to face him. "You should court someone else, Arthur. You know your family would never accept me and I'll not ever conform to fit in to make people happy. I will only bring you pain in the long run."

He frowned, the idea that she was not good for him an illogical notion. She was perfect for him. Never with anyone else did he have intelligent conversations, she was sweet and honest, unafflicted by the *ton*, nor was she poisoned by its many barbs.

"I think not." He leaned toward her and kissed her cheek. She smelled of lavender, fresh as a spring morning. "I feel I'm falling in love with you, if I have not already." The despair that crossed her features at his declaration made his gut clench. "Why won't you let me love you?"

She shook her head vehemently. "Please trust me when I say that we cannot go anywhere. It's not fair for either of us if we continue this liaison."

"I'm not fickle, Hallie. I'll not leave you again. I promise." The day he'd left her in Felday was one mistake that he'd not make again. Ever. He would fight to keep her, fight to make her his wife. "Trust me, please," he begged, not the least ashamed to. He'd do more than that if only it meant she would give him a chance.

"You're so maddening," she said, giving him a small smile. The first today. The sight of it warmed his heart and he grinned back.

"What are you reading about?" he asked, looking down at the book she held in her arms, wanting to change the subject and make her forget whatever concerned her regarding them.

"It's a book on the Roman Empire. I was sketching another coin that I found yesterday and I wondered if it may have been locally minted, not brought in from abroad.

If this book is saying what I think it does, the Romans did do this after their conquest."

"How much more do you have to do at the site? There are only a couple weeks left of the house party."

"Ah, but you forget I'm not here for the house party, you are. I'm free to stay as long as the dig takes. The original estimate was three months." A shadow entered her eyes, before she blinked and it was gone.

What was worrying her? There was something, he was sure of it, just as he was certain she was keeping something from him. In time he hoped she would trust him enough to confide in him.

"Whatever will I tell Baron Bankes to keep him from sending me away when everyone leaves?"

She chuckled, lifting her legs to lean on her knees. "That you're having an illicit affair with his archaeologist and you are unable to leave just yet."

"So we're still having an illicit affair? How daring of us." He reached out, needing to touch her. He ran his hand about her waist, wishing there were less clothes between them. He longed to feel her soft skin, to hear her sweet sighs of pleasure as he brought her to climax.

"If you will not listen to reason when it comes to us, then I suppose my only choice is to let you get your fill of me and move on. Is that not what most men do?" She reached out and cupped his cock. Arthur groaned at the contact and her boldness. Damn it, she was so perfect.

"I'm not most men." He placed his hand over hers and moved her hand downward, stroking his already hard dick. "For all the fun we may have together, I'm not going anywhere." She would see that was true soon enough.

*H*allie's stomach clenched at the feel of him. All masculine perfection and hers to play with if she wanted. Even if it were not forever, she could certainly have him while he was here for the house party.

Their future was impossible, but here and now was not.

She moved and straddled him, easy to do since she was wearing breeches. His hands came around and clasped her bottom, pulling her hard against his engorged cock. Heat spiraled through her and she could feel herself grow damp. Hallie moved against him, seeking her own release and pleasure without taking him into her.

His mouth twitched into a wicked smile and she kissed him, reveling in his need of her, his promises of forever. Promises that she knew could never be, no matter if they pulled at a part of her that longed for stability, for protection for her son and herself.

"You feel so good in my arms."

She moaned through the kiss as a tremor of pleasure coursed through her. "So do you," she managed. Hallie undulated against him, their breeches the only thing that separated them. That they were doing this in Baron Bankes's library was not the smartest idea, and yet she could not leave. Not now. She wanted to take her pleasure and forget all her troubles for a moment at least.

"I want, you." Arthur broke the kiss. He kissed her jaw, working his way around her neck and up to her ear, biting her lobe. "Damn these breeches."

Hallie pushed harder against his manhood, as she undulated in his lap and his breath hitched. His engorged cock was delicious against her and she could take her fill without too much fuss. Nor did she care how much noise they made. Everyone was out, and those who had stayed behind had better places to be than the library. Spasms started low in her core and blossomed throughout and she threw her head back, enjoying the climax as it tore through her body. He kissed her sigh of relief from her lips, quelling the noise. Hallie sagged in his arms, laying her head against his shoulder as they both tried to regain their breath.

"That was very pleasurable," she mumbled against his shoulder, placing a small kiss at the base of his neck.

His rock-solid phallus twitched against her and she sat back, meeting his gaze. "Did you not find release?"

He shook his head, swallowing. "No, but I want you to come to my room tonight. Will you?"

Hallie nodded without thought. She would take all she could of him for the time both she and he had left here. All too soon it would be over and she would have to find new employment. Funds that would have to be handed over to Mr. Stewart. A little distraction before life's realities was just what she needed.

"I will join you when everyone is abed." The thought of sleeping in his arms warmed her soul and the night couldn't come soon enough.

CHAPTER 14

*H*allie received a letter from her cousin later that day and she was relieved and pleased to hear Ammon was doing well and had started to learn his letters. A stab of disappointment that she was not the one teaching her son how to read and write pricked her conscience, but then she reminded herself that her working enabled him the comfort that he now lived in and supplied all the things he needed to learn and grow.

That was until the reality of Mr. Stewart and his blackmailing put everything she'd been working hard toward at risk. She could not allow him to use her in such a way. There had to be a way in which she could be rid of him.

She wrote back, telling them of all her finds and even drawing a couple of sketches of artifacts that she knew Ammon may enjoy, being a boy and liking military things. What boys did not?

After sending down her letter to be posted the following day, Hallie ordered a bath and prepared herself for bed, dismissing her maid early as she did not want anyone here later this evening when she snuck out to join Lord Duncannon in his room.

Her stomach clenched at the thought of being with him again. She hadn't thought to ever desire another man, but here she was, with the first man who had ever touched her soul and his wickedness, his determination to win her was a pleasure hard to deny.

A knock sounded on her door and she opened it to see Willow, her face stricken.

"Willow, come in. What is wrong?"

Willow looked up and down the passage and then, coming into her room, shut the door and locked it. "You will never believe the gossip I just heard before I retired for the night."

Dread lodged in her stomach and she clasped her abdomen. "Gossip? What is it?"

Willow's lips thinned into a disapproving line. "There is talk below stairs that a couple were caught *in flagrante delicto* in the library earlier today. Mr. Stewart says that he saw them with his own eyes. He did not know I could hear when he was telling Baron Bankes all the details otherwise I'm sure he would not have said a word." Willow paused for breath. "I know most who were out on the walk with the baron today, but there were several people who stayed behind. Lord Duncannon was one of them and so were you."

Her friend's direct inspection of her made her stomach churn. Hallie raised her chin, refusing to break under her friend's stare. "Mr. Stewart ought to be ashamed in telling such tales. I'm sure he would not like people talking about him if he found himself in that position." Hallie inwardly seethed. How dare he start such stories about anyone, not only her. It proved her unease correct about him. He was determined to bring her down, and not just financially.

"Oh, I'm sure he would not. Even so, it will not stop him from talking. He seems quite the gossiper."

Hallie yawned, hoping Willow would notice her need for sleep, even though she had no intention of sleeping, not for the next few hours at least. She wanted to see Arthur and tell him of what Willow had said. Perhaps he could speak to Mr. Stewart to ensure the man didn't spread rumors about them. That he knew they were in the library it was clear he understood what had happened between them.

Heat bloomed on her face over their actions and she cringed. If she did not have enough troubles already to worry about, now she had this to contend with.

Willow reached out and touched her arm, bringing her attention back to her friend. "I will bid you goodnight. I can see that you're tired. Goodnight, Hallie."

"I will speak to you in the morning. Goodnight." Hallie shut the door behind Willow and slumped against it. She glanced at the mantel clock that ticked just past the midnight hour. She would give it another half hour and then sneak over to Arthur's room.

Hallie sat in the chair before the fire to wait out the time. She watched as the flames licked the wood, it's flickering lulling her to sleep.

~

With a gasp she awoke, sitting up to the sounds of the maid opening the curtains and the sound of birdsong in the trees outside her window. A pot of tea and some toast sat on a silver tray on the small table before her, a pot of strawberry jam to the side that made her stomach grumble at the sight of food.

"Damn it," she mumbled, rubbing her face to try to wake up. How could she have missed spending a night in Arthur's arms? She swore under her breath, rolling her stiff shoulders at having slept in a chair instead of a bed. A very comfortable bed with a hot, sensual man who only wanted to please her at her side.

Hallie quickly ate and dressed, her breeches, shirt, and jacket making her progress a lot quicker than had she worn a dress. As usual, she headed for the servants' stairs, wanting to slip away to the dig site without seeing Mr. Stewart or Baron Bankes, whom she was wondering if she'd ever be able to look in the face again, especially now that he knew some of his house guests were enjoying each other.

If he learned it was her and Lord Duncannon she would not be offered any work anywhere else. He would make sure of that.

She stepped out the back door, glancing up at the cloudless sky and breathing deep the crisp morning air.

"Good morning, my dear."

Hallie stifled a scream and clasped her throat, heart beating a loud drum inside her chest. "Lord Duncannon. You're up early."

"Sleepless night," he teased and she couldn't help but chuckle.

"I'm sorry about that. I fell asleep." She continued toward the back-gate entrance of the yard, and could see a carriage was hitched at the stables. Panic assailed her that Arthur being up and the carriage hitched meant that he was leaving. "Will you be joining me up at the dig site today?" she asked, hoping the carriage was not for him.

He shook his head, pulling on his gloves. "No, unfortunately, but then neither will you. I want you to come on a ride with me."

"On a horse?" She was never overly fond of the animals, certainly not when she was on top of them and the idea of riding about all day wasn't something that tempted her.

"No, in the carriage. I want you to visit my estate. I'm neighbors with Baron Bankes, if you were not familiar. I have a proposition for you."

The mention of a proposition was intriguing and she studied him a moment wondering what he meant by it. She glanced toward the stables and saw Greg and Bruce waiting for her. Decision made, she went over to them.

"I'm going to visit Lord Duncannon's estate today. I'll not be needing you up at the dig site. We'll meet up there tomorrow at seven if you're free."

They tipped their hats. "Of course, Miss Evans. We shall be there tomorrow instead."

She smiled her thanks. Walking back, she gave Lord Duncannon her hand and he helped her climb into the carriage. She settled herself on the leather squabs, watched as Arthur joined her, seating himself beside her. The carriage was similar to what her friend and now the Duchess of Whitstone traveled in. Hallie didn't possess such a vehicle, having to travel about England by stagecoach, only having such luxury as this when she was with her friends who were well-to-do.

His lordship shut the door and rapped on the roof with his fist. The carriage rocked forward and he slipped off his gloves, placing them beside him. Hallie took in his strong, large hands. Without warning, his fingers entwined with hers and he held her hand.

She glanced at him, and yet he was studying the outdoors through the window, a serene expression on his face. Warmth spread through her at the sweet and innocent gesture, simply to hold her and be close without anything else insinuated.

Hallie wished it could be so easy as this. Just a joining of two people who liked each other, possibly even more than liked if her emotions were to believed. And if what Lord Duncannon had said in the library the other day was true.

"What is it that you wished to show me at your estate? What is this proposition you speak of?"

He smiled. "Well, as to that, I have a surprise for you that I think you'll be most pleased with." He shrugged. "I also wanted to show you my estate, my home."

She would be a liar if the thought of seeing where he lived didn't intrigue her. Was his home as warm as Arthur was turning out to be? A beacon of light that she couldn't help but warm herself against and chase away the chill of her worries?

They traveled in silence for some time and within an hour the carriage rocked to a halt, no sign of any home. Hallie leaned forward and looked out the window, seeing nothing but a dense area of trees in a shallow valley below. "Why have we stopped?"

His mischievous grin made her smile. "You'll see," he said, opening the door and helping her outside. They walked down the hill toward the trees and Hallie looked about, wondering what he was going to show her. As they entered the trees, the shadows chilled her skin and she rubbed her arms, wishing she'd brought a shawl. Arthur glanced at her and then, the gentleman he was, shuffled out of his coat and placed it about her shoulders.

"Thank you," she said, pulling him close and leaning up to kiss him. They were alone here, the servants on the carriage could no longer see them and his sweetness deserved a little something. Even if it were only a kiss.

He wrapped his arm about her waist and they continued on, coming to a low stone wall. "This," he said, gesturing to the wall and the others she could see, some taller as if they were an exterior wall to a castle. Hallie could see a fireplace, still blackened from the coal and past use. Beech and elm trees grew throughout the structure.

"It is the original site of our ancestral home. Cadding Castle was built during Henry the Seventh's reign and fell into disrepair when my great-great grandfather decided to build a bigger and much grander ancestral home, Cadding Hall."

Hallie ran her hand over the large stone blocks, could only imagine how imposing and large the castle would have been. She walked around the stone wall and into the center of one of the bottom rooms that no longer had a roof. She turned to face him. "It's very grand, but why did you want me to see this?"

"Well, as to that." He came about the stone wall and joined her, looking at the ruins with interest. "I'd like you to excavate the ruins. I want to rebuild the structure, but I would like any history of the site catalogued and preserved. I thought that if I had someone who knew what to look for, you may be able to help me rebuild it. Preserve it."

For a moment Hallie wasn't able to reply. She had not thought he would offer her such a proposition, but she could also not do the work for free. She would need laborers and equipment. This was a large job and would take months to complete. Did Lord Duncannon mean to pay her a salary, or was he hoping she'd do this for free?

"I'm honored, truly, but…"

"I will pay you handsomely. I'm not sure what the going rate is for an archaeologist, but I'll pay whatever you think is fair. Five hundred pounds, a thousand. Name your price and I shall pay it."

Hallie shut her mouth with a snap. "I do not need that much, my lord." The thought of such sums would help her secure her son and she would not have to look for more work unless the position was something that interested her. That is, if she could cheat Mr. Stewart out of what he claimed was his right to have.

While this was an interesting job proposition, she couldn't help but wonder if he were doing it to keep her close. Keep her in his bed for a little while longer. Not an awful idea, but still, being near him, day after day, night after night would only sink her further into that pit of emotions she'd hidden away for so very long.

"If I were to do this I need a promise, a declaration and contracts signed so everything is above board."

"Of course," he said, coming over to her and taking her hand. "I will admit to wanting you with me, but this rebuild has been in my plans for the estate for some time. I have the drawings already drafted, I just need someone to ensure the property or anything found here is protected from damage. Anything that was part of the original structure I'd like to include back into the build if possible. That's where you come in."

All of it made sense…but still… "I insist that I'll be given a cottage or a small building nearby to stay in. Our bed hopping has to end while I do this. I don't want to be talked about as your live-in lover who is being paid for her work at the dig site during the day and paid for my time in your bed during the night."

He ran a hand through his hair, looking about the ruins for a moment before he turned back to her. "Very well. I'll have you installed in a nearby cottage that my old groundsman used to live in and we'll keep our relationship purely business until after you've completed the dig here. But after that," he said, stepping up against her and wrapping his hands about her waist. Hallie relaxed against him, loving the fact that he made her feel so very at home, safe and adored. "I'm going to continue to court you, Miss Evans and nothing will stand in my way."

Hallie linked her fingers behind his back, wishing it could be so. "I think we have an agreement, my lord."

"And your price?"

She took a calming breath, thinking of her son and reminding herself Lord Duncannon said he would pay anything she asked. "I ask for one thousand pounds for the work I'm about to undertake, plus labor hire and tools." She held her breath as he contemplated her fee.

"Done," he said without question. "I'll have the money to you tomorrow."

She gasped and he took the opportunity to kiss her. Hallie forgot all about the dig, the money, everything, and gave herself up to his affection. She would have to tell him after she finished her work here everything of her past and let herself either live or die by the sword he could wield over her soul.

CHAPTER 15

True to his word, Lord Duncannon asked for a meeting with her in Baron Bankes's library the following day. They had spent a wonderful day at his estate, walking the grounds, seeing his home, the many family portraits and secret passageways.

He met her at the door and helped her into the chair before the baron's desk. "I have everything you asked for. I even had my steward write up a contract overnight and express it here this morning."

Hallie took the parchment from him and read through the contract, noting the amount to be paid, the support she asked for during the excavation prior to his building work to commence. Everything she'd asked for he had completed. She glanced up and saw another package tied with string. Her payment perhaps?

If Mr. Stewart found out how much he paid her, all of her negotiation and acceptance of this work would be for nothing. Overnight she had debated this dilemma and had decided that paying Mr. Stewart some of the money to keep him happy and quiet would be better than paying him nothing at all. It would still leave her ample money to finally take her son into her own care and move back to Felday. To be selective with the work that she wanted to do in future.

"It all looks very good, my lord. Quill please," she said, placing the contract on the desk, ready to sign. Arthur grinned, dipping the nip into the ink and passing her the quill. Hallie signed and with her scrawl of signature a little of the weight of having no security, having to rely on others for positions to keep the wolves at bay eased. This was the start of a new beginning. She sat back, meeting his gaze. "I'd like for the specifics of the contract to remain between us, my lord. No one needs to know the particular details of our agreement. Do you not agree?"

Arthur nodded without hesitation. "Of course." He pushed the package tied with string across the desk. "One last detail. Here is the one thousand pounds we decided on, delivered today as promised."

She picked it up, turning it in her hand, having never held so much money in her possession at any one moment. "Thank you. That is very generous."

He stood and came around the desk, dipping the quill once more and signing his part of the contract, then, rolling it up, turned and handed it to her. "Once you've completed your work here, I look forward to having you at my estate, Miss Evans."

She stood. "I do too." Which was true. She could not wait to be out from Mr. Stewart's watchful eyes and with any luck, with the money she would give him today, he would leave her alone for a little while.

"I must go, I'm already late heading up to the dig site."

"Of course," Arthur said, bowing. "Will I see you tonight?" he asked as she turned to leave. Warmth blossomed low in her belly and she bit back a small grin. "When everyone is abed, I'll come to your room. I won't fall asleep this time. I promise."

He grinned. "I'll count the hours."

Hallie walked from the room, an absurd little smile on her lips and hope in her heart. There was more between them than just physical attraction. He cared, she was sure of it. But did that mean he cared enough to want her when he knew everything? More importantly was she strong enough to tell him the truth and risk her heart a second time?

❧

*L*ater that day, Hallie sat in the tent at the dig site, eating a sandwich and waiting for a shower of rain to pass. Greg and Bruce had asked to return to the stables due to a mare who was in labor. Hallie had waved them off without hesitation and continued studying the small artifacts that had come out of the second trench. Half a statue that may be one of the many gods the Romans prayed to and more pottery pieces. The site was certainly of interest, but Baron Bankes had only wanted a small excavation to prove that there was once a Roman fort here. If her work here these past weeks proved anything it was that most certainly there was. At least she had proved the Baron and his family's thoughts on the site correct, even if she had not been able to make the site give up all its historical secrets.

"Miss Evans, just the woman I wish to see."

Hallie jumped at the sound of Mr. Stewart's voice, a voice that was both nasally and grating on one's nerves all at the one moment. "I hear you've been hired to work at Lord Duncannon's estate after finishing here."

She frowned. How had he found out? She'd asked Arthur not to say anything, and yet, here was Mr. Stewart not two hours later querying her about it. "Who told you?"

He smiled, the action more like a grimace. "I have my ways, but that's not important. I will tell you that Lord Duncannon did not bestow the information."

As pleasing as that news was, still, having Mr. Stewart here meant he knew some of the agreement. "I suppose you want your share."

"Of course," he said, seating himself across from her at the table.

Hallie took in his hair, a little oily and slicked back over his head. He reminded her of an eel, slimy and untrustworthy. She stood and went over to a box that was hidden in one of the tool trunks in her tent. It was not where she left such valuables, but she also had learned to carry her valuables with her at all times. If she were up at the dig site, so too was her money. No matter how great or small that sum.

She quickly took out the two hundred and fifty pounds she had separated earlier, closing the money box and the lid to the trunk. "Here you are. This is what I've been paid, minus one hundred pounds that I kept for myself. I cannot work and not have any money, so if you wish to fleece me of my funds, you must accept that I will be keeping a little for myself."

He rubbed his jaw, not taking the money from her outreached hand. Hallie schooled her features, trepidation edging in on her at his continued stillness. "And the rest of it?"

She swallowed, frowning for good measure. "I don't

know what you mean," she lied, hope that she may have tricked him fading.

He chuckled, the sound weary. "Ah, Miss Evans. I know you were paid one thousand pounds. So I would suggest you go back to the little money box in that trunk of yours, fetch out the six hundred and fifty pounds owed to me and do it quickly before I change my mind and take the one hundred pounds I'm willing to let go."

"How did you know? Tell me." She glared at him, all hope for her plans burning to ash before her. Her life with her son where they would not have to scrimp and save for every penny gone in a flash. That she would not have to take on multiple jobs such as what she'd done before Baron Bankes had offered her this position.

As much as she loved history, learning and exploring past lives through excavation, the position was hard work, hard on the body and tiring. Ideally she'd pick and choose the locations to explore and be paid fairly for it so she may be home most of the time, raising her son as best she could.

"I was in the library when you had your meeting with Lord Duncannon. Totally by chance as it was, but timely for me. Had I not been I would not have known you were trying to thieve from right under my nose. In future I will have to watch you more closely."

Anger spiked through her and she wrenched up from her seat, the stool she sat on falling down behind her. "Surely nine hundred pounds is enough for you that you do not need to keep blackmailing me. Is that not enough? I cannot do this forever."

"As I said before," he said, his tone bored and indifferent. Did the man have no heart? No moral compass? "You will keep paying me until I say otherwise. I'm looking forward to enjoying what this money can purchase me."

"You bastard. That is my life you hold in your hands. My son's future with me. His mother. You're taking that from me."

He pouted at her words and the urge to scratch his eyes out grew. Hallie clasped the table's side lest she do as she wanted. "So very sorry for you, but you did assist the Duchess of Whitstone on snuffing out my cousin's life. When you look at it, this revenge is all very equal. You hurt my family, and now I shall hurt yours."

"I did nothing to your cousin. Any bad tidings that happened upon him were brought on by himself." The vision of Mr. Stewart blurred and she blinked, hating that she was upset and he was seeing her so. She went back to the trunk and counted out another six hundred and fifty pounds, slamming it onto the table. "Get out."

"Oh, do not cry, my dear. You're a tough, working woman. You should be pleased you're able to help your fellow man," he said, sweeping up the money, his eyes greedy little beads at the blunt in his hands.

"What is going on here?"

Hallie gasped and swiped at her eyes as Lord Duncannon entered the tent, confusion written across his features until he saw the wad of cash Mr. Stewart was holding. If murder had a look, his lordship was the essence of that word.

"Nothing," she blurted, "Mr. Stewart was just leaving."

"With your money." Lord Duncannon strode about the table and ripped the money from the gentleman's hand, the man's mouth pulled into a displeased line. "What are you doing taking the payment from Miss Evans?"

Bile rose in Hallie's throat and she thought she may be

sick. She needed to tell Arthur of her past, no one else. He would hate her for lying to him. For others to know of her past before him. For giving him false hope.

Mr. Stewart adjusted his coat in an unhurried air. "In truth I've been blackmailing her. No point in not telling you everything if you wish to understand."

Arthur glanced at her, confusion and anger simmering in his blue orbs. "Why would you do that to her?"

"Because as I was just reminding her, she was involved in my cousin's death, Lord Oakes if you recall."

He frowned, before his eyes widened at recollection. "The bastard who almost raped and killed the Duchess of Whitstone?"

"The very one," Mr. Stewart said as if this was of such importance that it was worthy of such actions.

"Are you mad?" his lordship asked Mr. Stewart, staring at him as if the man had sprouted two heads. "This is not the behavior of a gentleman. You ought to be strung up for such underhanded, illegal business."

Mr. Stewart merely raised his brows, glancing at Hallie. "Perhaps Miss Evans would like to explain how it was that I've been able to blackmail her. Miss Evans," he said, "Do tell his lordship everything."

Hallie looked between them, warring with herself with the need to flee or stay and fight. The urge to flee rode hard on her heels, but she knew there was little point in doing that. Lord Duncannon needed to know the truth, she had just hoped he had not found out this way. Certainly not through the urging from Mr. Stewart, who seemed to be taking pleasure from both their pain.

She took a steadying breath, clasping her hands before her to stop herself from fidgeting. "Mr. Stewart has been blackmailing me because he knew of my past. My life in Egypt."

"I know of her life there, and yet you do not see me treating Miss Evans in such a way."

"You do, do you?" Mr. Stewart glanced at his lordship in surprise. "You know all of it? Everything?"

Lord Duncannon looked between them, doubt creeping into his gaze. "I thought so."

"You thought wrong," Mr. Stewart said, laughing and clapping his lordship on the back. Mr. Stewart headed for the tent exit. "I shall be off then, this little tête-à-tête has made me quite famished. I believe dinner will be served within the hour. Nothing like a little disagreement to warm the blood and make me salivate."

"Hallie?" Lord Duncannon said, pulling her attention back to him. "What happened in Egypt?"

Mr. Stewart popped his head back into the tent at the question. "She had another man's child, my lord. Thought you knew." He shrugged. "I must have been wrong. My mistake."

Hallie met Arthur's gaze and read the confusion and hurt within his stormy, blue orbs. She stepped toward him and he held up his hand, halting her progress.

"You're a mother!" A look of repulsion crossed his features and she raised her chin, not willing to be looked down upon, not even by the aristocracy.

"I am a mother. I can see by your face that this disappoints you, my lord, but if you expect me to apologize for my life I will not."

"You said… I thought you said there was no one in Egypt."

"I never said that, I merely did not tell you there was. You made your own summarisations on my situation. They were wrong." She was being unfair, and cruel, but then she had to protect herself now. No one else would do it.

He rubbed a hand over his jaw, looking out toward the dig site. "The child is not mine, is it? That night in Felday. You did not get with a child."

"No, my son is not yours. He's a man's named Omar whom I met in Egypt."

His lordship's eyes widened and he stepped farther away, as if being near her was akin to being near someone who had leprosy. "Your child is half-Egyptian?"

She nodded, having no shame in that. "Yes he is. He's living with my cousin at present. Once I'm finished at Baron Bankes's estate I planned on traveling there to spend some weeks with him. He's only four, you see."

"I do not believe it," he stated, his face one of disbelief. "How could you not tell me such a truth? Were you ashamed?"

"I'm not ashamed of my son, but I'm also not a fool. I know that my options of positions like this or even as a servant in a great home would be compromised if they knew I had a child out of wedlock. I need money, my lord. I do not have a dowry or great estates that would earn my income and keep me well pleased and placed in life. That is the reason I chose not to tell anyone of my past. For capital reasons only, not moral."

"You allowed me to believe there was a chance for us. How could you do such a thing?"

She swallowed the lump in her throat at his words. So he was throwing her aside without hearing the whole story, her truth. Not even willing to see her side or to trust in the feelings she had thought he had for her. "I tried to dissuade you, to tell you that a future with me was not possible. You would not listen."

"I did not mean… It was one thing for me to overlook your status in society, the fact that you would come to the marriage with little compared to my wealth and property. That is what I thought you were concerned about. I did not care for that and would have ignored my grandmother's bouts of melancholy over our marriage, but I cannot overlook this. You are a mother. A mother to a child who is born out of wedlock."

"You're no better than Omar. We've been intimate and a child could have been made. How is this any different? Is it that you're a lord and Omar was not, and that makes it alright?"

He ran a hand through his hair, leaving it on end. "It just *is* different."

Hallie sat back down at the table and picked up her small brush that she used to take the mud off of artifacts. "I guess we're done here then." She would not fight for a man, a life with a man who had double standards. If he would change his mind about her simply because she had birthed a child, he was not the man for her.

Tears pricked her eyes and she blinked for everything that she'd lost. If Omar had lived, she possibly would not be in this situation, even though his family too were against the union. Had, in fact, refused to consider such a thing. It was probably for the best. She would finish up here, return and collect her things tomorrow and go home. There would be other positions she would get, if Lord Duncannon did not tell everyone of her past. "Are you going to tell anyone?"

"Of course not," he said, staring down at the ground as if it would give him some magical insight. "I gather Mr. Stewart found out about your past. How much was he exploiting you for?"

"He had," she answered, seeing little point in keeping anything from him now. "He found out about my son, about Omar. He threatened to tell everyone everything so no one would hire me, not as an archaeologist, historian or servant," she told him, matter-of-fact, trying to keep her emotions in check. Her throat physically hurt at holding her feelings in order and she'd be thankful when he left.

She glanced at him and found him watching her, his face a mask she could not read. "In light of what you've told me, I see now that you will be unable to work at my estate. I will however give you the money, that's yours to do with as you will. Mr. Stewart will not get his thieving hands on that blunt."

"I do not want your money or charity, my lord. Please leave." She picked up the cash, handing it to him. "You know everything there is to know about me and my life and have said yourself that you're not interested in any of it. I think we both know there is little left to say to each other."

"I am sorry, Hallie. Had the circumstances been different…"

She nodded, not game enough to look at him. "Goodbye, Lord Duncannon."

"Goodbye, Hallie."

At the sound of his retreatment, she looked up and watched him walk down the hill, back toward the estate. She slumped back down into her chair, swiping angrily at the tear that snuck down her cheek. She would finish up her position here and then leave. She no longer wanted to be here, or anywhere near where Lord Duncannon was or his hypocritical ilk.

CHAPTER 16

$\mathcal{A}$rthur returned to Baron Bankes's estate and, spying a footman, ordered his things to be packed and a carriage be ready within the hour. He paused mid-word to the sound of a woman's shrieking, authorative voice. He inwardly groaned, recognizing the voice of his grandmother.

What the bloody blazes was she doing here?

"I demand to see my grandson. Where is Lord Duncannon?"

God damn it. This was the last thing he needed right at this moment. His mind was a jungle of thoughts and denials of over what had just happened. Hallie was a mother! He could not wrap his mind around it. Anger thrummed in his veins that she'd lied to him, kept such important and personal details about herself secret. Did she not feel anything for him? Certainly it proved she did not trust him.

He started up the stairs for the first-floor drawing room. Guests of Baron Bankes's house party milled in the hall and some were also in the drawing room, all of their attention set on his grandmother and her demands.

"Where is Duncannon? He needs to answer to me and this news I received. Where is this vixen Miss Evans who thinks to make herself a countess?"

"My lady, you're mistaken," Arthur heard the baron say, trying to placate his grandmother with a soft tone. It would not help. The woman knew only one tone and that was abrupt.

"Miss Evans is employed here to do an excavation of my Roman ruins. She's in no way seeking marriage with Lord Duncannon."

Arthur made the door, seeing his grandmother wave a missive in the air. "This is not what this letter states. I demand to see him at once. Where is he?"

"Right here, Grandmother," he said, coming into the room. "Everyone leave, thank you."

"Have you offered for Miss Evans? The historian who has birthed a child out of wedlock? A child to a foreigner? An Egyptian no less." His grandmother clasped her chest, searching for a chair before seating herself down with the aid of two female guests who looked in no rush to leave.

"We will speak of this alone."

"Oh, no we will not. There is nothing to speak about," she said, her jowls vibrating with each word. "You're not marrying any hussy. The next Countess of Duncannon will be a lady of good birth and breeding. Why, any one of these young women present will do. I'll not have my grandson bringing the family name down for a common tart who should be working in St. Giles instead of digging up dirt in Somerset."

"Do not speak of Miss Evans in such a way, Grandmother. I'll not have it. No matter what your thoughts are on her past." *Or his.* Arthur glanced at the many faces who had heard everything about Hallie. She would return here to a pack of wolves, all waiting to take a bite out of her.

He turned to Baron Bankes. "Send word for Miss Evans's things to be packed up. You can see as well as I that she cannot stay here."

"I will do it," Willow said, stepping forward from behind some of the other guests, her disdain for him written plainly across her features. Willow's aunt looked at her charge, her face ashen with the news his grandmother had told them all.

"You'll not go near Miss Evans again, Willow. I forbid it."

"She is my friend, Aunt. I shall ensure she is protected before she leaves. Unlike some here, I do not forget my friends or those I care about," she said, looking directly at him.

Her words shamed him and he fought not to cast up his accounts. "Thank you, Miss Perry."

She turned to him at the door, glaring at him. "I do not do this for you, do not fool yourself on that account, my lord. Neither do I wish to ever see your spineless self again near my friend. Did everyone hear that?" Willow said, her voice peaking an octave or two. "Or do you wish for me to repeat it?"

Arthur watched her storm down the passage, her skirts flying about her ankles. Her steadfastness toward Hallie shamed him further and he inwardly swore. "Everyone. Out. Now," he yelled, startling the few about him. They scrambled from the room.

"I will ensure Miss Evans leaves today. We cannot have that sort in our homes. What will everyone think?" the baron said, clucking his tongue and shutting the door, leaving Arthur with his grandmother.

"How could you be so irresponsible, Arthur? You know our family do not, ever, marry anyone that is not the finest, best bred, accomplished, and has a good dowry and from a respectable family. You will uphold tradition, and you will cease any contact with this Miss Evans. Whoever heard of a woman historian, or one who goes about digging up ancient piles of stone that no one cares about?" His grandmother rolled her eyes, clutching at her diamond necklace about her neck for support. "Your parents would turn in their graves should they see you now."

Arthur slumped into a nearby wingback chair, wrecked over what had just come to pass. He did not care that his grandmother was voicing her concerns, she could've gone on for months and she would not have swayed him from his choice of Hallie.

He shook his head. The thought that she was a mother unimaginable. She had never once slipped and mentioned her son or the man that she'd loved enough to bear him a child.

His hands fisted at his sides. The urge to punch something, anything, riding him hard. He hated the bastard, whoever it was who loved her. If the fellow loved her so very much why did he not marry her, bring her home and look after her and their child? Had he abandoned them in Egypt?

He groaned, having not thought to ask her why he was not with him.

"Are you listening to me, Duncannon?"

His head snapped up to look at his grandmother, her face a mask of disapproval. "What were you saying?"

"You're to leave and return to Cadding Hall tonight. Baron Bankes is as we speak going to set out to remove

Miss Evans from his home. After I explained to him that for a baron to be around such a woman would not do his reputation in London any good, he saw the sense in this advice and will act accordingly."

Anger rode hard on Arthur's pride and still, the thought that Hallie would be kicked out as if her time here was worth nothing at all made him seethe. To be removed in disgrace simply because she had chosen a different way of life to those under this roof.

He stood. "I'm going to my room to pack." With nothing left to say to his grandmother or anyone for that matter, Arthur strode back to his room, ignoring the few who congregated about the drawing room door, no doubt listening in on his conversation.

A woman stepped in front of him and he reached out, grabbing her shoulders lest he tumble them both to the ground. He looked down into the steely-green eyes of Miss Willow Perry.

"How could you act such a coward toward Hallie? From what I can gather here today, you now know of her past and disapprove her choice."

His lip curled. He was not in the mood for a lecture. "There would be few who would not disapprove. Am I wrong?" he asked, glaring down at her since she continued to glare up at him. She sniffed her displeasure.

"Let me ask you this, my lord. How many women have you slept with in your life? I should imagine it would be many and yet women are not afforded the same freedom. Well," she said, jabbing him in the chest with her finger. "Hallie, Ava, me, hell, all our friends are not going to conform to a man's rule, even if this is a man's world. And if you're not man enough to accept and love Hallie for all that she is, then you do not deserve her."

"I guess I do not." The words rose up his throat and threatened to choke him. Still he could not accept what Hallie had done. What Willow said was true, he'd slept with a lot of women since first sampling a lovely lady's maid in his mother's employ before she passed. The idea, however, of his wife having been free with her body, her heart, left a sour taste in his mouth and he couldn't stand the thought of Hallie being with someone else.

To have had his child...

Yes, he'd slept with her, but he was going to marry her. If only he had been the only man to have ever entered her bed.

"Do not ever try and see her again, my lord. I'll not allow you to hurt her again."

"Is she back from the dig site?" Was Hallie back in the house already? If so, the baron was quick in having her services ended. The idea hollowed him out inside. Damn it!

"She is packing. The baron told her not half an hour ago that she was to leave due to everything your grandmother shouted out to half the *ton*."

"In my defense I did not know my grandmother was arriving today." His only relative wasn't even expected at the baron's home, so for her to be here, word of his attachment to Hallie had to have reached her side in London...

He clenched his jaw, thinking of only one person who would wish to cause her harm.

"Your excuses are not relevant. Leave her alone, marry a young, rich, *pure* debutante that has her maidenhead intact. One that your family are so famous for aligning themselves with and leave my friend alone. She deserves happiness and you and your toxic grandmother will only bring her pain."

Arthur stood silent, very little words coming to mind to retaliate against Miss Perry. How could he when everything she said was true?

He bowed. "I intended to, Miss Perry. There is no need to lecture me."

She scoffed, walking back up the passage toward Hallie's room. "Remember what I said or you'll not just face me, but Ava and our friends. And I can promise you, *my lord*," she said, his title full of sarcasm. "You think your grandmother is a tyrant, you haven't seen anything yet."

$\mathscr{A}$ knock on the door sounded and Willow, who had been helping her pack, unlocked it and wrenched it open. Hallie couldn't help but look to see who was there, a little part of her hoping it was Lord Duncannon who had come to apologize and beg forgiveness.

Not that she would ever forgive him for his treatment or yet worse, judgement of her. Who was he to look down his nose at her simply because she had followed her heart? She doubted very much that he could say the same. There was little doubt that he had slept with many women, none of whom he was in love with, so who was worse? Certainly, it was not her.

Her maid over the past couple of weeks stood at the door, a missive in her hands. "Miss Evans, an express came for you this evening. I'm sorry it took me so long to bring it to you. I did not know you were back from the dig site." The young maid's eyes darted about the room, seeing her clothes and trunks out. "Are you leaving, miss? Do you need help?"

Her stomach pitched at the sight of the missive and she

all but forgot her troubles with the baron, Arthur, even her maid's question. Hallie took the missive and broke the seal, scanning the letter. Words of *illness, return home, post-haste* jumped out from the text and she stood motionless a moment, her mind a whirr of plans.

She started when Willow closed the door, speaking softly to the maid about a carriage and two footmen to help before coming over to her. "What is it, Hallie?"

"I must go at once. My cousin is ill."

"The one who looks after Ammon?" Willow strode back to the trunks and started packing them less carefully than she was before. "I've ordered you a carriage and a couple of footmen will be here soon to help carry the luggage down. We'll have you on the road to Berkshire before the hour is up."

"I do not think the baron will allow me to have the carriage all the way to Berkshire. I'll have to take the stage-coach from the nearest town."

"Leave that with me. I'll make sure you're safely delivered to Berkshire by tomorrow. I may only be a niece to a viscountess, but that doesn't make me entirely without merit. After what has happened to you today, you will not be dumped at the local inn to find your own way home. I'll not have it."

Hallie pulled her friend into a hug, so very thankful that she still had her true friends and that they would support her, no matter what. She should have trusted in that friendship when she found herself with child. No longer would she hide in the shadows, scared of what people would think of her or her choices. She would pretend to be the widow of Omar El Sayed, the mother of his child and everyone could go to the devil if they did not like that.

"Thank you, Willow. You are the best of friends."

"I am, and will always support you." They smiled at each other a moment before Willow patted her shoulder. "Come, more packing." She turned to a nearby trunk, throwing some of Hallie's boots into it. "Does the missive say very much about your cousin? How severe it is?"

"A severe fever and she's very ill. They're unsure if it's contagious. I hope Ammon does not get it. I would hate anything to happen to him. He's only a child."

"All will be well, my dear. I'm sure her friends have a doctor attending her."

Hallie tried to take comfort in her friend's words, but the mention of a fever that seemed to be affecting her cousin's mind made her fear the worst. What if she passed away? Whatever would she do then? She had not saved enough to keep her and Ammon secure in Felday. She had her friends, of course, to turn to, but they could not support her forever. After the atrocious way her truth came out here at the baron's estate, it was highly unlikely she'd ever gain such employment such as this again, or even work in a great house as a maid.

Her name was, or would very soon be, mud.

Hallie rubbed a hand over her brow, her hand coming away a little damp from perspiration. At least the baron had paid her in full for the work that she had done, and with no sign of Mr. Stewart she had not had to hand any over to him. Not that she had to worry about his black-mailing self any longer. Not now that everyone knew the truth.

The next hour was a blur of her trunks, missives to Greg and Bruce in the stable of her thanks to them, and where to forward her tools and paperwork, sketches and equipment that she had left up at the dig site. She had asked the footmen to take her things downstairs using the servants' staircase and to have her depart from the stables. She did not wish to see anyone from the house party, or the baron who had caved like a rock under pressure when Lord Duncannon's grandmother demanded he shun and fire her.

Hallie did one last turn about the room, ensuring she'd not left anything behind. She turned and picked up her pelisse and woollen cap that she preferred to wear. Willow watched her, her eyes a window of disappointment and Hallie took her hands, squeezing them. "None of that. I will do as you say and keep my thoughts positive regarding my cousin. I'm sure she will be well, and she'll get better even quicker when I'm there."

"I will miss you. We'll be leaving next week back to London, so please write me and tell me how your cousin fares and of course, yourself."

"I will. I promise." Hallie started for the servants' stairs, her steps slowing as she caught sight of Lord Duncannon waiting for her in the passageway.

"You're leaving."

It wasn't a question and she nodded, anger spiking through her blood at the sight of him again. What did he think he was going to achieve seeing her again? He'd made his opinions clear enough up at the dig site. She certainly did not need them to be repeated.

"I am. If you'll excuse me," she said, pushing past him and starting down the stairs.

"Hallie," he called after her. "If things were different..."

Hallie adjusted the small valise in her hand, ignoring him. She swallowed the lump in her throat that his words placed there. No more tears, no more heartache. She would return home, get her cousin healthy again and then return to Felday. Forget the Viscount Duncannon and bury everything he made her feel and want.

There was only one man in her life from this point onward. Her son. The rest could go to the devil. Sooner rather than later.

CHAPTER 18

*H*allie reached Berkshire and her cousin's home the following afternoon. Thankfully Willow was true to her word and Baron Bankes's driver had taken her right to her cousin's door and helped unload all her trunks into the house.

The one, female servant her cousin could afford helped get her things inside. "How is Charlotte, Betty? Where is Ammon?" she asked, untying her bonnet and placing it on a nearby sideboard. Her cousin's home was larger than her cottage at Felday. Her only relative had married a gentleman farmer and after his death on the farm, had been left with the income from the land and the house. With no children of her own, she had been happy to help Hallie when she returned home, pregnant and with no support. Hallie owed her so much. In truth she would never be able to repay her kindness.

"She's upstairs, Miss Evans. Ammon is sitting with her. He wanted to tell her everything that happened at school today."

Of course, it was a Wednesday and Ammon would

have attended the local parish school. He was only four, and yet he was bright for his age. "That is good that she's up and talking. I had thought it was much worse than that."

"Oh, no, Miss Evans. It is merely a trifling cold." The maid glanced over her many trunks. "Are you staying for some time, Miss Evans? I will have the guest bedroom set up if you are. I do apologize, but we weren't expecting you."

Hallie frowned. They weren't? "Please, if you will. I'll be here for several days." Hallie started up the stairs. How could they have not expected her when they had written the missive?

She knocked on the wooden bedroom door and heard Ammon, his little excited voice telling of a story about a tree and his friend who had attempted to climb to the top. "May I come in?"

"Mama!" Ammon jumped from his chair and ran toward Hallie. She kneeled down, taking him into her arms and hugging him fiercely. His little hands clutched about her throat, and tears sprung into her eyes at having him near her again. No longer would she leave him behind. It wasn't fair on either of them. Somehow she would find work and be able to keep him close.

"Oh, I've missed you, my darling," she said, pulling back and taking in his sweet face. Eyes, the same as Omar's, stared back at her and made her miss him all the more. Miss what could have been. "You've grown. You'll be a young man all too soon."

Ammon stepped out of her hold, standing taller at her words. "Auntie thought so too. Miss Smith had to let down my pants. My ankles were showing."

Hallie chuckled, picking him up and going to sit on the

bed, placing her son on her lap. Not wanting him too far away from her. She turned her attention to her cousin. "How are you, Charlotte? I received a letter saying you were very ill. Is this true?"

Charlotte shook her head, a confused mien on her face. "We never wrote to you at all, except a fortnight past about Ammon and what we've been up to. I have a cold, but not severe enough that you should return home."

"How odd." The pit of Hallie's stomach churned as she tried to figure out who may have sent the letter. "If you didn't send it, I wonder then who did."

"Ammon, why don't you go down to Miss Smith. I'm fairly certain she told me at lunch that she made a sweet treat for you today."

Ammon looked over his shoulder to Hallie. "May I, Mama?"

She leaned down, kissing his cheek. "Of course, my darling. I will join you downstairs soon."

He ran off, the sound of his small footsteps on the stairs making Hallie smile. "Sending Ammon downstairs, I assume there is something you wish to tell me, Charlotte?"

Her cousin's mouth thinned into a displeased line. "There have been some people in town, staying at the inn. They're Egyptian and I've seen them watching Ammon when I pick him up from the parish school. It's too coincidental. I think they know who he is."

A chill ran down her spine and the urge to run downstairs, pick up her son and keep him safe and in her vision at all times thrummed through her veins. "Does Miss Smith know to keep an eye on him?"

"Of course. She was the one who actually mentioned it to me first." Charlotte frowned. "Do you think they're here to take him away?"

"I'll not let them go anywhere with my son, but I also refuse to live in fear. I shall go to the inn today and see what their presence is about. I'll not have our family feel threatened, not by anyone."

"Good, very good," her cousin said, reaching out and clasping her hand. "I've grown so fond of the boy, I'd hate for anyone to take him away from us. Even if they are his father's family." Hallie nodded, trying to hide the fear that thrummed through her veins. If Omar's family was here, it meant only one thing. They knew he'd had a child and wanted him in Egypt.

~

*A*rthur sat in the carriage, almost back in London, the houses on the outskirts of the city passing him by. He took little notice, his mind a whirr of thoughts, of regrets mostly on how he'd handled the situation with Hallie.

He'd let her down, turned his back on her when he should have stood behind her, a pillar of strength and support. He ought to be horsewhipped for judging her. Why was it all very well for men like him to bed whomever they pleased and whenever they wished? Hallie had not done such things, but instead had given her heart to a man in Egypt and had mothered a child.

He cringed, laying his head back against the squabs. No matter how much she hated him right at this moment, she could not hate him as much as he hated himself. He'd not just let her down, he'd let himself down too. The Lord Duncannon was not a gentleman who judged, not anyone. Life was for living, for loving and enjoying. From the moment he first met Hallie, her desire for life, to live and

TAMARA GILL

see the world told him of a soul that would not be tamed, and he did not wish her to be. He'd known that about her, it was one of the reasons he loved her, and yet, he'd thrown that back in her face, told her in a roundabout way that her life was scandalous and beneath his. That she would not make a proper wife.

"Fuck it," he said aloud.

His grandmother's eyes grew uncommonly wide, her face turning a ruddy red. "Arthur, I beg your pardon. Do not blaspheme in front of me. Not now or ever."

"Why not?" he asked, staring at her. He shouldn't blame his grandmother, she was a product of her time, a woman who had an opinion on everyone, no matter if it were wrong or right. "I've fucked it right up and will never be able to repair the damage I've done."

She sniffed, rolling her eyes and stared out the window as if the king himself was outside and keeping her attention. "I suppose you're talking of Miss Evans. The trollop."

"She's not a trollop. I'll not have you talk about her like that."

"I shall talk about her in any way I please. Unlike you, I did a little investigating on her before coming to fetch you from Somerset. Did you know that her child is the sole heir to the late Omar El Sayed family in Egypt? I had a very interesting letter from a gentleman who had taken an interest in Miss Evan's life. Another jaded lover no doubt, but he did impart some very interesting information. One tidbit that he'd written to her lover's family in Egypt telling them of the child. They are en route to collect the boy, or so I was informed last week."

Arthur's blood ran cold at his grandmother's words. "Was this letter informing you of this by any chance from a Mr. Stewart?"

"Why, yes it was. Do you know of him?" she asked, seemingly excited by the chance that they both knew the man. By god yes, Arthur knew him and when he got his hands on Mr. Stewart he would strangle him so he could not cause any more trouble. "You may not care, but Mr. Stewart has been blackmailing Miss Evans for some weeks. Threatening to disclose her son, ruin her chances of earning an income all because he's the cousin of the late Lord Oakes, the very gentleman who tried to kill the Duchess of Whitstone. I doubt very much the duke would look favorably on anyone who aided such a man." Arthur watched as his insinuation was understood by his grandmother, her face paling. "Let us not forget that Miss Evans is the close friend of the duchess as well."

His grandmother's eyes narrowed. "Threatening me, no matter how vague you are being with words, will not work, my boy. You must admit your mistakes and move on from them. Miss Evans may have been a little diversion for you while in the country, but over my dead body will I allow her to become the next Countess of Duncannon."

"What if I want her to be my wife? Will you accept that and mute your viperish tongue? I would hate to have to send you to the country. And please, my dear Grandmama, understand my words are not a vague threat, but a promise of what is to come if you cause any more trouble."

"You're going to marry her! How could you do that to your family? The Duncannons do not marry fallen women. You'll bring the whole family down into the pits of scandal and debauchery."

He shrugged, having heard enough. "I love her. I have always loved her, even before she left for Egypt and I thought I'd never see her again. I find that I do not care about her past, only that I want to be in her future. If she and her son will have me." Never a bigger question to be asked. He would fight to keep her in his life, and if that meant he would become a father to her child, then so be it. He would not turn away from anyone whom she loved. Not even another man's child.

Some would call him a fool, turn their backs on him and some doors in London would be forever closed to them over his choice and yet he did not care. Let them close their doors, he knew there were some who would forever give admittance and that was enough. They were his true friends.

"I forbid it, Arthur."

He raised his brow at his grandmother's voice that brooked no argument. "When I drop you in London I'm going to continue onto Berkshire and win back the woman whom I adore, and nothing that you or anything that society says will change my mind. I'm happiest when I'm with her. I need nothing else."

She pointed a knobbly finger at him, her face pale. He was sorry for causing her such pain, but he knew the truth within himself. This was the right course. His body thrummed with expectation for his life to start and he knew who he wanted at his side when it did.

"I will never admit her to my home. Nor any children that you have. From this point forward you're dead to me."

He sighed, shrugging. "Well, that is a shame, Grandmother for I am the viscount and head of the family and as thus I control the money that supports the family. If you punish Hallie for a life lived to the fullest, I shall punish you in the same way. Is that what you really want?"

"How dare you, you insulant boy!"

The carriage rocked to a halt and Arthur glanced

outside to see they'd pulled up before his grandmother's Mayfair townhouse. "I will write to you the details of my wedding. I expect to see you there."

His grandmother alit from the carriage, and huffing her discontent, stormed up the townhouse front steps. Arthur watched as she pushed the door open, not giving the butler time to get out of the way, making the man stumble.

Arthur shook his head, yelling out directions to Berkshire and settling back in the squabs. If they traveled through the night and changed the horses regularly he should reach Hallie's cousin's home by dinner tomorrow, perhaps a little later. His task to beg for forgiveness would not be an easy feat. Hallie would not be easily swayed that he was sorry, but he was. So sorry that his chest ached every time he thought of living a life without her.

He would not lose this war. He would win her and her love. For him, there was no other choice.

CHAPTER 19

*H*allie walked into the taproom of the local inn later that afternoon, the venue eerily quiet and without its usual customers. She was thankful for the little brass bell that was above the inn's door, for not a moment after she'd walked into the room, filled with tables and a fire, well alight and filling the room with warmth and cozy ambiance, a short, but stout man walked in behind the bar. Hallie smiled, hoping her politeness would help her in making the publican disturb his guests and bring them down here to talk to her.

"Good afternoon, sir. I'm hoping to speak with some guests staying here, I understand. They're not English and perhaps have a thick accent. Do you have anyone who's staying her similar to that?"

"Oh ay, we did, miss, but they've rented the late Sir Garrick's estate just north of the town. If you follow the road that leads back to London, make a left about a quarter mile up and you'll come to the estate quick enough."

"Was there a woman who was part of that party?"

The publican rubbed his bearded jaw, pulling down on his tuft of hair as if stroking some sort of animal attached to his face. "No, there were two gentlemen, very well dressed, but no lady that I know of. They only stayed one night here before they were able to take up residence at the estate.

"Thank you for your help. I shall go there directly."

Hallie went back into the hitching yard at the inn and using a mounting block, jumped up on the back of her cousin's only mount. She patted the horse, hoping the beast didn't let her lose her seat. It was times like this that she wished she was as good a rider as Ava. Unfortunately, it was not a specialty of hers.

She made her way up the north road and turned left when she came to a well-worn road, the roof of the estate just visible over the tree tops. Nerves pooled in her stomach at the thought that the people there may well be Omar's family, his mother or father. They were such a wealthy and influential family in Egypt. Their presence here only meant one thing. They had learned of Ammon and wanted him.

Never one to deny people what they wanted, she of course would allow visitation to Ammon. Had Omar not warned her against contacting them, she would have done this herself, but he'd made her promise that their union be a secret. His family, he explained, would never understand his love for her or hers for him. Hallie had kept that promise, but perhaps with Omar's death, his parents had mellowed. Losing a child changed people, maybe it had changed Omar's family in regards to their thoughts on her.

It only took a few minutes before she pulled the horse up to the front of the house, tying her mount to the front step railings. The place looked deserted, no sign of gardeners or staff about the property. She glanced up at the building, a shutter on a window hung haphazardly from its broken hinge, and the steps looked like they'd not been swept for some months.

Hallie wrapped the brass knocker on the door, a hollow echo running throughout the house before the clipped footsteps of someone inside met her ears. She took a calming breath, ready to discuss and negotiate with Omar's family if need be, but she would not crumble under that great family's pressure.

The door swung wide and she stumbled back, fear spiking through her. "Mr. Stewart. What are you doing here?"

He stepped outside, his pace cautious as if she would bolt at any moment. The thought had crossed her mind, but the fact that she wasn't a fast runner and her horse was currently tied up behind where Mr. Stewart stood, the option seemed pointless.

"Miss Evans. I thought you would come. You're a clever woman, I will give you that."

She frowned, confused by the turn of events. She'd expected to see Omar's family here, but then maybe… "You made it appear as if my son's family were here from Egypt. Perhaps it is I who should say that you're a clever man. A cruel one too I should think."

He chuckled, the sound laced with menace. "Oh, I'm all of those things. I did do as you said. Made it look like your son's family were here to collect. But even I cannot get word to them quick enough that I found out where your son was, or have them here to take him away from you. I have, however, sent word to them, so I'm sure in the future your son will be well cared for. As for you, that's another matter."

"What do you mean?" She edged back and he followed like a lion stalking its prey.

"I hope you made your goodbyes with your son because you'll not be seeing him again." He clasped her arm, wrenching her toward the door. "Do come in, my dear. I've prepared a room especially for you."

Hallie tried to tug free, but his grip, punishing and stronger than she thought it would be given his wiry frame only tightened. "I'm not going anywhere with you."

"I'm not going anywhere with you either. I'll be leaving here today, but you, my dear will be well received downstairs in the bowels of the house. This place was owned by the late Sir Garrick. Their family is currently arguing who will inherit the house and lands. The disagreement shall go on for some months I'm sure, plenty of time for you to wither away and starve to death alone and in the cold. Just as you deserve since you helped snuff out the life of my cousin."

He pulled her toward a door that had it not been open Hallie would not have seen. It melded into the paneling of the room when closed and if he placed her down there, no one would hear or look for her in such a place. No one other than the publican knew she was here, and she'd not given her name.

Panic seized her and she twisted from his hold, slipping on the dusty parquet floor as she tried to run for the door. Her skirts, damn them to hell, caught on her legs and she fell to her knees. Mr. Stewart grabbed her from behind, hoisting her up against his front. "Shhh. Shhh, my dear. You'll only be hungry for a few days. After that you'll merely grow weak and tired. Eventually you'll not wake up at all. I could set the house on fire, give you an ending like my cousin, but I'll take pity on you and won't do that. I'm not that much of a monster."

He laughed at his own words and Hallie fought to remain calm. Not to panic. She stomped her foot hard against the top of his, and he let her go, swearing. Hallie took the opportunity to run, this time her focus on her feet and legs, making sure they remained upright and steady.

Pain sliced through her head as he clasped her hair, pulling her back. She landed with a thump on the floor, her head snapping back and sending her vision to blur.

He came over her, clasping her jaw and squeezing her mouth until the coppery taste of blood ran onto her tongue. She whimpered. "Do not attempt to escape again, bitch. I'll not be so kind next time."

Tears blurred her vision and he tugged her up onto her feet, pushing her toward the door that led down to the cellars and who knew what else. The staircase down was made of stone and looked to be a lot older than the structure of the house itself.

"Is your clever mind wondering if this is the home's original cellar?" He glanced at her, his easy smile and politeness back again instead of the deadly ire and loathing she'd read in them only minutes before. How a man could be so changeable was impossible to fathom and something she did not want to be around ever again. Not that there was a chance of that with her being buried alive down here.

"There once stood a castle here, during the eleventh century I believe. The cellar is all that remains and when the house was constructed they simply built over the existing footings. Perfect for you, my dear. As you're wasting away, you may study it if you like. I'm not so barbaric to leave you in the dark. I have supplied you with candles so you may see during your stay. Are you not pleased?" he asked, smiling.

Hallie clamped her mouth shut and kept her hands still at her sides lest she scratch his eyes out. The bastard was mad. As mad as his cousin. There must be some kind of disorder that ran through the family for these cousins to act out in such a mean and deadly way.

The thought of Lord Duncannon flittered through her mind, that she would never see him again. That her beautiful son would never know where his mama went or why. The stairs spiraled ever downward and even if she were to yell out for help until her voice was hoarse, no one would ever hear. This was in effect a tomb. Her tomb.

How fitting indeed since she'd spent her life studying the dead in places such as these and now she was going to be one of them.

Mr. Stewart had lit some sconces on the wall that showed them the way until the sight of a wooden door, leading into a room at the end of the corridor, revealed itself. Hallie rubbed her arms, the dark closing in about her, threatening to send panic to spiral through her mind. She would not succumb to panic. To panic meant death. Probably sooner rather than later.

Her cousin would send out a search party. She would find her way here. This was not the end. Mr. Stewart thrust her into the room, slamming the door closed. One candle burned in the corner and she raced over to it as the sound of steel locks sliding into the stone outside.

"Goodbye, Miss Evans. I do wish you a pleasant death," she heard him say, his voice muffled by the thickness of the door.

Hallie went about the room with the candle, searching the space for any way out, for more lighting. Fear turned her blood cold and she shivered. He'd left her one candle after all his talk of not leaving her in the dark, and nothing to light it with. She was going to die. Alone and in the dark. She leaned against the wall, her knees feeling all of a sudden less than steady and she slid down to sit on the floor.

The stone scratched at her back but she didn't care. There was no way out of this mess. She bit back a sob and fought not to cry. She was a strong woman, intelligent and brave. She would not give in, not now. If she was here in a week and still no one came, then she may lay down and wait to die, but until then, she would fight like hell to remain in this world. As unkind and unfair as it was at times, it still beat being entombed and buried alive like she was right now.

❧

*A*rthur made it to the small village of Slough the following afternoon just as the sun started to drop in the eastern sky. He asked for directions in town and a young woman carrying a basket of bread and other food-stuffs pointed for him to continue along the road he was on until he came to the small, thatched-roof cottage on the outskirts of town that Miss Evans's cousin resided in.

At the nearby inn that he'd checked into earlier he had ordered soup, bread, and cheese to be packed and taken up to the residence just in case it was needed. He wasn't sure what was going on, or at least the severity, but the maid at the inn had mentioned a Mrs Nibley, Hallie's cousin had taken ill a week or so ago and was doing poorly.

Arthur came to the cottage that had a large front door and two windows on either side. It was quaint, but not as tiny as he'd thought it would be. The garden, mostly vegetables, looked well-tended, the windows sparkled clean in the afternoon sun. He knocked on the door, dread curdling his blood that Hallie would be displeased he had followed her. That she would not see him and send him away.

He could well understand that. He would not be impressed if the situation were reversed. Her wrath he deserved more than anything, he just hoped that from that pain and disillusionment they could rebuild a life. Together as a family. He would not let her son's family take the boy away from her. Not after all she had done to keep him safe and protected.

His grandmother's words had haunted him this past day, and he could not help but fear that he was already too late. That Mr. Stewart's evil vendetta had already marked its victims and her son was lost to her. On a boat headed east. Arthur stood before the red door.

He took a fortifying breath and knocked. He fixed his cravat as the door swung wide, but instead of there being a servant or Hallie opening the door, a small boy looked up at him, his large brown eyes taking in his every feature and sizing him up. The boy was undoubtedly Hallie's, he could see her features in the boy's face, forever curious to know more. Something in the region of his heart squeezed and he kneeled, smiling to try to put the young boy at ease.

"Hello, I'm Arthur Howard, Viscount Duncannon. I'm wondering if Miss Hallie Evans is here."

The young boy shook his head, but opened the door wider.

Arthur stepped inside and took in the home. It was as clean and well kept on the inside as it was on the out. The small sitting room that the front door opened into had a large, roaring fire and comfortable-looking settee with a floral pattern on it. He went over to the hearth and stood before the flames, warming his back and hands.

The little boy ran off toward the back of the house and within a moment the steady beat of footsteps sounded on the polished wood floor. "Can I help…" a young woman's words faltered at the sight of him and she frowned.

He took her in, her modest morning gown that was a little thread worn and covered in an unflattering apron. Her hair was askew and looked as if half the pins were missing. Even so, he could tell she was a relative of Hallie's. He was doomed to see people, it seemed, who reminded him of the very grave mistake he'd made. Of losing the woman he loved.

"I'm Lord Duncannon."

"I know who you are, my lord. Miss Evans is not here."

Her abrupt answer was more than he deserved, but he needed to speak to Hallie. To beg forgiveness. Promise her everything she'd ever wanted, if only she would be his. Be his wife.

"I'm looking for her. A matter of great importance that if you're willing, I thought to speak to you about." He glanced at the small boy and smiled as the little boy's mouth gaped up at him, watching the interaction with enthusiasm. Arthur winked at him, smiling as a small grin tweaked the boy's lips. "Alone if you're willing, Miss Nibley, I assume."

"Mrs Nibley." She glanced at the small boy, turning him to meet his eyes. "Go into the kitchen and help Miss Smith with the biscuits. I'm sure they're almost ready to go into the oven." She gestured for Arthur to sit on one of the settees in the room, before seating herself, adjusting her skirts and meeting his gaze. "What do you want, my lord?"

"First, I have come to apologize to Miss Evans, but to also tell her of what I've learned of her son's family. I believe they may be on their way here from abroad to take the boy. I need to warn her."

Mrs Nibley leaned forward, her hands clutched tight in her lap. "They're already here, and I do not know what to do. Are you in Hallie's confidence? You know everything?"

The question shamed him. He was in Hallie's confidence to a point, but then had shunned her like everyone else would eventually do at her past. He cringed. He was the worst of men. "I was, and I wish to be again, if she'll forgive me. But please tell me what you know. Maybe I can help before anything is attempted."

"We've seen men about town. Men that are undoubtedly foreigners. They have been watching Ammon for several days. The men had been staying at the local inn and Hallie went there yesterday. The publican told her of the house these gentlemen had rented outside town, on the north road to London and she went there. I know she did for I found my horse wandering the grounds the next day, but I cannot find her, or the men.

"There is no trace of anyone at the house. The property was the late Sir Garrick's. The family are arguing over the inheritance, and the house has not been lived in for months. It certainly would not have been leased to anyone, so for the publican to tell me that is where the gentlemen went makes no sense."

A chill went down Arthur's spine as he took in this information. His grandmother had said Mr. Stewart had written to Omar's family, but that could take months to reach them and then for them to act on such news. But they were here now. They had either found out about the child by other means, or Mr. Stewart was lying and was behind Hallie going missing.

"Where is this house?"

Mrs Nibley stood, striding to the kitchen, stripping off her apron as she went. "Miss Smith, I am taking Lord Duncannon to Sir Garrick's estate. We think we may find what we're looking for there."

"What are you looking for, Aunt?" the young boy asked, looking up at her with interest. Arthur watched as she reached down, cupping his cheek. "Is it Mama? She said that she would take me fishing before she leaves again."

Anger thrummed through Arthur's veins that if Hallie had been injured, had been taken away from her son and himself he would kill whoever removed her from his life. Mr. Stewart better be miles away from them, for when he caught up to the fiend, he would be lucky to survive the assault.

"Your mama will be home soon. I promise. Now, off you go and help Miss Smith. I'll be back shortly."

Using Arthur's carriage, Mrs Nibley gave directions out to the house and within half an hour they were pulling up before the large, imposing home that was in need of some repairs.

"This is where I found my horse wandering about yesterday," Mrs Nibley said, pointing to the overgrown lawns before the estate. "I have written to her friends from school for assistance after not being able to find her. I'm hoping they will be here within a few days to help look for her here or in London. It's so out of character for Hallie to do this. I cannot help but think these two men we've seen about town have taken her somewhere. Why they would take her and not Ammon though I cannot fathom."

Nor could Arthur. It did not make sense. He tried the door and found it unlocked. Pushing it open he called out. Hearing no reply, he stepped inside, looking about the large foyer. "Hallie!" he yelled, stilling to see if he could hear her. He turned to her cousin. "Let's search the house and then go from there. I'll start downstairs, you go upstairs and search the bedrooms and servants' quarters.

"Very good." Arthur watched as Mrs Nibley ran up the stairs. He turned for the first room on his left, a library, the books left as they were from the moment of Sir Garrick's demise. The house would not be worth anything if the family continued to argue over it for too much longer. He called out to Hallie as he went from room to room, checking in cupboards and in locked doors that sometimes had to be forcefully opened. The kitchen had a small cellar, but that was empty, save for a few blocks of cheese that had been left to rot.

He turned in the cellar, walking up to the wall and feeling it. It was made of stone, large gray blocks. The house was made of sandstone, but looking at these walls surrounding him, the house was built on top of an older structure. A much older one at that.

Arthur raced back into the foyer, yelling out to Mrs Nibley who started down the stairs at his yelling. "What is it, my lord? Have you found Hallie?"

"Has this house always been here or was there once an older structure in this area?"

Her eyes brightened. "Oh yes, you're right. This estate was built on top of the foundations of an old castle."

They stared at each other a moment before Arthur recognized the moment Mrs Nibley had the same thought as he. Her eyes widened, reminding him of Hallie and making him miss her even more.

"A castle often has a dungeon."

"Dungeon," Mrs Nibley said at the same time as Arthur, looking about.

"It's not in the kitchen," he imparted, before going to the stairs and opening the door beneath the central staircase. The space was empty, save for a few cleaning rags and an old dusty broom. He came back into the foyer, looking at the floor. Perhaps a trapdoor?

Arthur frowned, noting the dust on the floor had been disturbed more than what they had done. He stepped to the side, inspecting it from another angle and followed the disturbance toward the wall where it stopped. "What the hell," he mumbled, going over to the wall and feeling the wood paneling. He felt along the beading, not feeling any little lever or lock hidden in the wood.

"Push the wall," Mrs Nibley said, joining him and pushing farther along the wall as if she hoped the wall would open.

He did the same and to his surprise the wall released and a door opened along the beading, revealing another door. Arthur grabbed a nearby candle, lighting it quickly with the flint beside it and held it into the black void.

Stairs…

"Hallie!" he yelled, not hearing anything in return. "Wait here, Mrs Nibley. If I do not return within the hour, go to town and get help. I'm not sure how stable and secure this old structure is. Best that you do not follow me."

"Of course," she said without question.

Arthur stepped into the ancient part of the building and started down the spiraling stairs that were worn in the center from hundreds of years of use. The air was cool, musty and water seeped through the stone the farther down he went.

At the bottom of the stairs, of which he thought would never end, he came to an open space that led into a corridor farther into the ground. He shook his head, hating the thought that Hallie could be down here. It was no place for anyone. Even Arthur felt the shiver of the past crawl over his skin and whisper to remove himself.

Up ahead, out of the dark a door came into view. He lifted his candle, not seeing any light coming from the space. "Hallie, are you down here?"

A rustling sound and then two loud thumps sounded on the other side of the door. He stilled, his heart pumping loud in his ears, before he heard the faint feminine scream of his name.

He bolted to the door, taking care not to snuff his candle before unbolting it and pushing it open. No sooner had he opened it, was he engulfed in a fierce hug, arms wrapped so tight about his neck that he thought he may pass out from lack of air.

Arthur lifted her out of the cell, holding Hallie close, rubbing her back and trying to stem her fear he could feel thrumming through her body. Her skin was chilled, and she shook in his embrace. "I'm here. I have you," he said, kissing the top of her head, cooing calming thoughts of being out in the sunlight in a few minutes. Of seeing her son again.

"My candle snuffed out and I couldn't see. I couldn't see anything." Her sob tore at his heart and he swore revenge on the bastard who had done this to her.

Tears sprang to his eyes and he took a calming breath, needing to be strong. "Come." He wrapped his arm about her waist, and picking up his candle, turned back toward the stairs. "Let's get you home."

"I would ask you how you found me, but you're right,

all I want is to get out of here, please. I just need to feel the sun on my skin and see my son."

"I know you do." They made their way upstairs and as they came closer to the foyer, the stairway started to come into view from the sunlight outside. "Almost there, Hallie. I'll not let anything happen to you. You're safe with me." He would keep that promise and he would find out whoever did this to her and murder the bastard.

CHAPTER 20

*H*allie woke early the following morning, the sun streaming through the bedroom window and pulling her from sleep. She rolled onto her back, her hip sore from lying on the cold, stone floor of the dungeon for almost two days. The thought of still being there, of no one ever finding her made a cold tremor run down her spine.

She glanced about the room, thinking of Lord Duncannon, only to spy him sleeping on a chair beside her bed, his head laying back against the seat, his mouth open a little in slumber. Even dishevelled as he now was, still he was the handsomest Englishman she'd ever met and yesterday when she'd heard her name being called in his voice, she could have cried with relief. Well, perhaps she did a little.

As if sensing her watching him, he opened his eyes, his blue orbs heavy lidded, his hair askew and sticking up in places. The urge to run her fingers through his blond locks and tame his mane overwhelmed her, and she contemplated those feelings and what they meant, even now, after their terrible disagreement.

"You stayed."

He rubbed his jaw with his hand, sitting up to lean on his knees. "How are you feeling this morning?"

Hallie sat up and leaned against the bedhead, pulling the blankets up about her chest. "I'm sore, my hip is bruised from sleeping on the floor and I think I've pulled a few muscles. I had a little altercation before being placed in the dungeon."

Arthur growled at her words. "Who did this to you, Hallie? I need to know."

"Mr. Stewart." The thought of what that man put her through left no impediment in telling Arthur everything. He deserved to know who it was and how it happened. This was not a secret she could keep from him. Never again would she keep anything from him. "He hired two men who appeared to be foreign to watch my son. Enough so that it became obvious to my cousin and her servant. They wrote for me to return home, but I had already left by the time the missive arrived. I had also received a letter stating my cousin was ill the same day the baron asked me to leave his estate. All lies that Mr. Stewart had concocted to get me to return to Berkshire."

He cringed at the reminder of his failure. "And then?"

"The men being in Slough made us all think that Omar's family was here. I went to confront them at the inn, but I was told they had leased Sir Garrick's estate. When I arrived I realized my mistake. It was simply another threat from Mr. Stewart and a means to get me alone. I never saw the other two men that my cousin had spoken of, so I think they were merely hired thugs. Mr. Stewart locked me in the dungeon with no intention of coming back. Had you not found me…" A shudder wracked her body. The thought of being buried alive, far under the ground where no one could hear her shouts for help made her stomach churn.

"I will kill him."

Warmth seeped into her bones at his intention to defend her. She watched him a moment, he too was looking at her, the concern and warmth in his eyes made her wonder if he'd had a change of heart. That he'd found her certainly made it look that way. "Why are you here, my lord?"

He stood and came to sit at the edge of her bed, taking her hand. "Because I was wrong. I should not have judged you as I did. I should not have placed what my family thought, of what society would think above what I felt. I've fallen in love with you. You would not be the first woman to have had a life before marriage. I will never hold it against you. I promise on my life that I will not."

Hallie studied their intertwined hands. "Your family will never accept me. It is bad enough that I'm poor and have no great bloodline to bring to your family, but I have a child. One born out of wedlock and one who is of mixed race. I'm not certain you're prepared for what that will mean to you and your family. Progressive as you may be, or trying to be, society is cruel and there are those who walk among it who will never welcome you again into their homes, or offer friendship to my son when the time comes for him to take his place in that world."

"I will fight every day for the rest of my life to ensure Ammon is treated with respect that is due to him."

"Will you really, Arthur? Or are you merely saying everything that I wish to hear? Back at Baron Bankes's estate, you told me of all the reasons why it would not work between us. I'm no fool. I know one of the reasons is because my son is born out of wedlock and to an Egyptian man. I will not allow you to resent him in time if others turn their backs on us. If you were to ever do that, no matter the scandal, our marriage would be at an end. So if you really mean what you say, you must truly, wholeheartedly mean it."

"I do, Hallie. To my very soul, I shall never let you down."

She wanted to believe him, but he was a lord, a viscount. Marriage to her would mean so many sacrifices. To give herself to him, to allow him to become her son's father figure in his young life was a gamble she wasn't sure of. She fiddled with her bedding, unable to meet his gaze. So many thoughts ran through her mind, his past words, Arthur's declaration now. Denial of all that he made her feel. Refusal to accept that her heart had been touched once again. All of it confusing and muddling to her mind.

The door to the room flew open and Ammon ran in, jumping up on her bed and wrapping his small little arms about her neck. She pulled him into her, breathing deep the scent of his hair. To have him back in her arms, to see him again was the best medicine for her sore muscles and bruised hip.

"Mama, you're back. I thought you had gone away again."

"I'm here now, my darling and we'll never be apart again."

He pulled back and she pushed a lock of hair out of her son's eye. He had his father's eyes, a rich brown with golden flecks that would forever remind her of the hot, Egyptian land. As if remembering there was another person in the room, Ammon turned to Arthur, smiling.

"Good morning, Lord Duncannon. Thank you for bringing my mama home."

Hallie watched Arthur's reactions to her boy, and saw nothing but sweet amusement and interest in his blue orbs. No calculation over what to do with him to remove him from view, to keep her son hidden from the social sphere they would circulate. Lord Duncannon simply looked at her boy, a sweetly mannered child who was happy to have his mother back and smiled.

"You're very welcome, Ammon. I told you I would bring her home, did I not?"

"You did. When Miss Smith explained to me what a lord was, I thought that you would not fail."

Arthur chuckled and Hallie smiled at their exchange. Her son, always the inquisitive boy, sat, legs folded on the bed and looked between them, his eyes narrowing in thought.

"You love my mama."

Hallie blinked to clear her cloudy vision that her son's question brought forth in her. Why she was teary over such a question she could not say. The fear that he would deny such feelings perhaps, or worse, state that he does.

"I love your mama very much, but I've been a fool these last few days and so you find me, Master Ammon groveling at your mama's feet, begging for forgiveness."

A grin tweaked her lips and she sighed.

"Mama, you should forgive. He looks sad and you always tell me that when people look sad we should try and make them happy. I think if you married him, he'd be happy." Her son nodded as if this was the very best idea.

"I think Ammon is correct. You should marry me and make me happy. And make you happy as well."

Hallie looked at her son, his sweet face alight with

hope. As for Arthur, his eyes had clouded with uncertainty at her continued silence. She bit her lip, confounded if she should risk her heart a second time. The memory of Arthur pulling her into his arms after finding her in the dungeon swam through her mind. He'd come for her. Had saved her from a terrible, agonizing death.

"Promise me that you'll never let me down, Lord Duncannon and I'll marry you."

He smiled as Ammon yipped with joy, clapping his hands. Arthur pulled her son into a celebratory hug and the tears she'd been holding back fell unheeded. Never had she seen her son be embraced by a man, and not any man, but her man. Her future husband.

Arthur searched inside his coat pocket, pulling out a small box before holding it up to her. "Marry me, my beautiful, intelligent, loving Hallie."

"Yes, yes, yes," her son cheered, giggling.

Hallie glanced down at the yellow solitaire diamond ring. Never had she ever seen anything so beautiful. She sniffed, nodding. "Yes, I will marry you, my understanding, loving and protective Arthur."

She smiled as he pulled her into a fierce embrace, kissing her soundly, heedless of anyone about them. Her son made a disgusted sound and she heard him run from the room, yelling out for her cousin.

"Ammon seems well pleased," Arthur said, as she reluctantly let him pull back.

"And so am I. I'm sorry I wasn't more honest with you. I promise to never keep anything from you again."

He wiped the tears from her cheeks with his thumbs, kissing her softly. "I understand why you did. I will never hurt you again, Hallie. Nor Ammon. I give you my word as a gentleman and a man who's adored you from the moment you stopped your carriage and glanced out at me as if I were a madman. I fell in love with you that day, and nothing has ever changed that emotion in me. I love you so very much." He pulled her against him, holding her tight. The familiar longing rose in her and she could not stop herself from kissing along his neck, up toward his ear.

"I thought you so handsome, so untouchable the first time I saw you. I think I too fell a little in love."

He groaned as she nipped his earlobe. "Only a little in love?"

"I told you that I would never keep anything from you again, or lie. I'm telling you the truth."

He pushed her back into the pillows, kissing her soundly. Heat thrummed through her and she could not help but wish they were alone, locked in a room and already husband and wife. "Hmm. Perhaps spare me those truths. A man does have his limits."

She chuckled, sliding her hand up under his shirt and feeling the corded muscles flex beneath her fingers. "You do?"

"I do, and let me be honest now, Miss Evans, you're pushing me to the edge of mine right now."

"Good, because you push me too." Not that she didn't love every moment of it.

EPILOGUE

Two Years Later, Somerset

Hallie heard the awful, loud bellow of an animal she'd not thought to hear emanating from their garden in Somerset. She pushed up from her desk where she was looking over the latest finds at the castle she was helping Arthur renovate and glanced out the window. "What on earth," she gasped, unable to believe what she was seeing.

A camel.

"What are you up to, my dear?" she mumbled to herself, watching with amusement as her son cautiously walked over to where Arthur was, standing beside him as the camel bent down to sit on the ground, two front legs first, followed by the back legs.

She rubbed her ever-increasing belly as the baby kicked, laughing as the camel gave out a mournful moan.

Hallie went to the doors leading out onto the terrace and pushed them open, going to stand at the balustrade. "Should I even ask what you're about, Arthur?"

He laughed, showing Ammon he had nothing to fear by touching the camel's neck. He called over a man she'd not seen standing aside. The owner of the camel she presumed.

Arthur kissed her as he came to stand beside her, wrapping his arm about her waist. "With our travels abroad planned in the next couple of years, I thought it necessary to show Ammon a camel. We'll be riding them, I have no doubt, when we get to Egypt."

She rolled her eyes, laughing at his forethought. "They have horses in Egypt, you know. Carriages too. We do not need to be riding camels."

He shrugged, his eyes dancing with amusement. "Where's the fun in that?" he said, throwing her a wicked smile that two years after their marriage still made her heart flutter and miss a beat.

Arthur had fulfilled all his promises he'd made to her that day in her cousin's home. He'd taken revenge on Mr. Stewart. Had hired a bow street runner and had the man arrested for bribery and kidnapping at a gambling hell one of Arthur's friends owned. A man Hallie had never met, but apparently had been friends with both the duke and Lord Duncannon since Eton.

Hallie couldn't help but feel sorry for Mr. Stewart living his days in Newgate prison. It would not be a place that she'd ever wish to be, but then whenever she had those thoughts, she reminded herself that all of what she had now would have been impossible if Mr. Stewart's plan had succeeded.

As for Ammon, well, Arthur had excelled as his step-papa. They were a pair to be seen about the estate. Always had their heads together, talking of books and horses, one of Ammon's favorite animals and one her new husband had gifted her boy upon their marriage. A gentleman always had a horse Arthur had declared.

Arthur lifted Ammon up on the camel and she clasped the railing. "I'm not sure that's a good idea. It's very high up there."

"No, Mama, it'll be fun."

With her heart in her mouth she watched as the camel stood, her son's eyes growing wide at the jerky action and height. "Hold on tight, Ammon."

Arthur came back over to her as the owner led him about the yard. "I have something to tell you."

Hallie kept an eye on Ammon, making sure he did not fall off. "What is it?"

"Ammon called me Father this morning at breakfast."

Hallie gasped, turning to look at Arthur. "He did?" Her vision blurred and she bit her lip, having never thought he would ever call anyone that term. They had been honest and told him of his father, of how brave and good he was. The letter Mr. Stewart had written to Omar's family did not evoke the response that he wished. In fact, the family responded with only one letter, disputing her claim and asking not to be contacted again. Hallie had been disappointed for Ammon who deserved to know where he came from as much as anyone, but she had expected that kind of reply. They had not welcomed her into their home when Omar was alive, it was unlikely they would now that he was gone.

"He did and that brings me to what else I have decided to do." Arthur picked up her hand, kissing it.

"Please tell me you're not going to keep the camel?"

He chuckled. "No, not that. But I have decided to have Cadding Castle bestowed to Ammon upon my death. That part of the land is not entailed and with it I shall include several thousand acres to support the estate. The castle will be rebuilt in a couple of years and I'd like to see it go to my eldest son, even if he is not mine by blood, he is mine in every other way. I want him to know that I love him as much as I will love the little child that we've created. I'll not see any of my children go without."

Hallie threw herself into Arthur's arms. How had she been so fortunate? "You're too good to me. Thank you, Arthur. Thank you for doing such a wonderful thing for our boy. If Omar were here, he would thank you for caring and loving Ammon when he could not."

He pulled back, clasping her face in his hands. "What is life if it is not for living, for loving and making those you love happy? I love you, Hallie, so very much. Ammon is not just your child, he is mine as well."

Hallie kissed him, deep and long. A heady ache thrummed in her veins and she wrapped her arms about his neck. If only they could go upstairs, disappear for a few hours... "I love you too. Thank you for being mine."

He threw her a wicked smile. "Thank *you* for saying yes. I always knew we'd be perfect for each other."

And they were...perfectly happy.

AUTHOR NOTE

As you've probably noticed, I did take some creative license in regards to my heroine being an Archaeologist/Egyptologist/Historian. Of course, during the Regency period, such positions were not open to her sex, but I wanted her to have the life she longed for.

Women have come a long way from being ostracized from these careers, but that doesn't mean that in the nineteenth-century women didn't tread a path for those who came later and wanted to explore and learn about lost civilizations and cultures.

Some of these women, whom I recommend you look up and admire are listed below.

Margaret Murray (1863-1963)
Gertrude Bell (1868-1926)
Gertrude Caton-Thompson (1888-1985)
Dorothy Garrod (1892-1968)

Dear Reader,

Thank you for taking the time to read *Hellion at Heart*! I hope you enjoyed the second book in my League of Unweddable Gentlemen series. Hallie was an interesting and fun character to write. I should imagine there were lots of women like Hallie who wanted to be more than a housewife. Oh to dream…

I'm forever grateful to my readers, so if you're able, I would appreciate an honest review of *Hellion at Heart*. As they say, feed an author, leave a review!

If you'd like to learn about book three in my League of Unweddable Gentlemen series, *Dare to be Scandalous*, please read on. I have included chapter one for your reading pleasure.

Tamara Gill

DARE TO BE SCANDALOUS

LEAGUE OF UNWEDDABLE GENTLEMEN,
BOOK 3

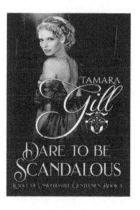

After inheriting a small fortune, Willow Perry has everything she's ever wanted. Except a husband, that is. But not just any husband will do. She's looking for a grand love—someone who will challenge and excite her. It's just her folly that the one man who interests her is a notorious rake. He's as wild and passionate as Willow is sheltered and staid. Love between such polar opposites would be impossible ... wouldn't it?

. . .

Abraham Blackwood has devoted his life to the pursuit of pleasure. He's perfectly happy to run his gaming den and ignore the expectations of society. But meeting the lovely Willow gives him another goal. Revenge. Making her pay for the sins her family committed against his will be easy. Ignoring how much he wants her—not only beneath him, but at his side, forever? That might prove to be infinitely more difficult.

When Willow discovers Abraham's true intentions, can the fragile bonds they've begun to form survive? Or will the cards remain firmly stacked against their happily ever after?

PROLOGUE

1826 London

Willow raced up her aunt's stairs, having been summoned back from her daily ride at Hyde Park. Sweat pooled on her brow, and she could feel it running down the line of her back beneath her gown. It was too soon. This day could not be the end of her aunt.

She ran as fast as her riding ensemble would allow and pushed open her aunt's bedroom door, coming to an abrupt halt at the sight of her lady's maid, the butler, and housekeeper, all of their faces masks of pity and sadness.

"Auntie?" She came and sat on the bed beside her, reaching for her hands. They were cold and limp in hers, and Willow squeezed them a little, needing to rouse her, keep her with her for just a bit of time longer.

"I'm still here, my child. I waited for you."

Tears pooled in Willow's eyes, and she clasped her aunt, her only family left in the world into an embrace, her throat as raw as if a hot poker had pierced her there, making each breath painful and hard.

"I'm so sorry. I went riding. I did not know that you were so poorly."

Her aunt shushed her, the action bringing on another bout of coughs that wheezed and rattled her chest. The hack sounded painful, and if her aunt's grimace each time she coughed was any indication, the infection was causing discomfort.

"I want you to go riding, even when I'm gone. You will have more time on your hands then. You won't have to trundle after me anymore."

That may be so, but Willow would have to trundle after someone. When her aunt passed, she would need to find employment, and soon. The thought brought her no pleasure, and her stomach churned at the prospect she would not find work. Not that her friends would leave her out on the street, but they had their own lives now, families to take care of, they did not need a friend latching on to them for charity.

"Never mind that," she said, not wanting to talk about what she would do after her aunt passed. The doctor had promised she had some weeks left, not one. Her decline had been so fast in the last few days. Too fast. Willow prayed for time to stop. For her aunt not to leave her alone in this world. "You'll be better soon, and we'll look back on this day and laugh. You'll see. Nothing to fear just yet."

Her aunt's lips twisted into a grin. "I wanted to tell you before I go what I've done." Her aunt squeezed her hands, suddenly stronger and capable as they once were. "You will have time, my dear. To finally do as you wish because I'm leaving you everything that I have. The London town-house, my estate in Kent, my money. All of it is yours."

Willow stared at her aunt, knowing full well her mouth was gaping. "You cannot. I'm not a Vance."

"No one is. With no children and no one to take on the title, I can do what I wish with everything else. The title and house in Norfolk will revert to the Crown, but nothing else."

"Are you sure, Auntie?" Willow asked. Surely there was more entailed than just the Norfolk property. She could not get everything.

"I will lose the house in Norfolk, but everything else is yours, my darling." Her aunt sat up a little, her eyes bright. "You have been a shining light in my world since Maurice died, the child that I never had. You are my sister's daughter, but you are mine as well. I want you to be safe, to be protected after I'm gone. Making you my heir accomplishes all this. I will rest easy knowing you will be protected."

"Oh, Auntie." Willow's vision blurred at her impossibly good fortune at a time when the loss of the woman before her would be too much to bear. "I love you so much. Thank you. It is too much."

Her aunt sighed, lying back on the bedding, a small smile about her lips. "I'm happy to." She reached up, touching Willow's cheek with her palm. "You will suit being an heiress, just try and keep some of the funds for yourself and not give it away to all the unfortunates. I know what a good heart you have."

Willow chuckled. Even now, as ill as her aunt was, she was making banter, trying to make her laugh. "I will try. I promise." Willow sat back as her aunt slumped into her bedding, her eyes closing with the exertion of having spoken the last few minutes.

She watched her, holding her hand. Her chest rose and fell, telling Willow she was still here. "I will miss you so much, Auntie. Thank you for loving me as you did. I will never forget your kindness."

The housekeeper came over to Willow and placed a comforting hand on her shoulder. Willow could not stop looking at her aunt's breathing. In. Out. In. Out. In. She waited for the exhale. It never came. Willow stood, clutching at her aunt's hand. "Auntie. Auntie," she cried, louder this time, but nothing. No breaths. No words. Nothing.

She turned to the housekeeper who stared at her, tears in her own old eyes. "She's gone to be with God, my dear. Come away now."

Willow did as they bade, unable to fathom what had just happened. Her aunt could not be gone. It wasn't possible. She paused at the threshold of the room, looking back at her only relative — the dearly departed sister to her mama. The Viscountess Vance. "I will miss you," she whispered, before leaving the room. "Always."

Want to read more? Purchase Dare to be Scandalous today!

LORDS OF LONDON SERIES
AVAILABLE NOW!

Dive into these charming historical romances! In this six-book series, Darcy seduces a virginal duke, Cecilia's world collides with a roguish marquess, Katherine strikes a deal with an unlucky earl and Lizzy sets out to conquer a very wicked Viscount. These stories plus more adventures in the Lords of London series! Available now through Amazon or read free with KindleUnlimited.

Lords of London

ALSO BY TAMARA GILL

Royal House of Atharia Series

TO DREAM OF YOU

A ROYAL PROPOSITION

FOREVER MY PRINCESS

ROYAL ATHARIA - BOOKS 1-3 BUNDLE

League of Unweddable Gentlemen Series

TEMPT ME, YOUR GRACE

HELLION AT HEART

DARE TO BE SCANDALOUS

TO BE WICKED WITH YOU

KISS ME DUKE

THE MARQUESS IS MINE

LEAGUE - BOOKS 1-3 BUNDLE

LEAGUE - BOOKS 4-6 BUNDLE

Kiss the Wallflower series

A MIDSUMMER KISS

A KISS AT MISTLETOE

A KISS IN SPRING

TO FALL FOR A KISS

A DUKE'S WILD KISS

TO KISS A HIGHLAND ROSE

KISS THE WALLFLOWER - BOOKS 1-3 BUNDLE
KISS THE WALLFLOWER - BOOKS 4-6 BUNDLE

Lords of London Series

TO BEDEVIL A DUKE

TO MADDEN A MARQUESS

TO TEMPT AN EARL

TO VEX A VISCOUNT

TO DARE A DUCHESS

TO MARRY A MARCHIONESS

LORDS OF LONDON - BOOKS 1-3 BUNDLE

LORDS OF LONDON - BOOKS 4-6 BUNDLE

To Marry a Rogue Series

ONLY AN EARL WILL DO

ONLY A DUKE WILL DO

ONLY A VISCOUNT WILL DO

ONLY A MARQUESS WILL DO

ONLY A LADY WILL DO

TO MARRY A ROGUE - BOOKS 1-5 BUNDLE

A Time Traveler's Highland Love Series

TO CONQUER A SCOT

TO SAVE A SAVAGE SCOT

TO WIN A HIGHLAND SCOT

HIGHLAND LOVE - BOOKS 1-3 BUNDLE

A Stolen Season Series

A STOLEN SEASON

A STOLEN SEASON: BATH

A STOLEN SEASON: LONDON

Time Travel Romance

DEFIANT SURRENDER

Scandalous London Series

A GENTLEMAN'S PROMISE

A CAPTAIN'S ORDER

A MARRIAGE MADE IN MAYFAIR

SCANDALOUS LONDON - BOOKS 1-3 BUNDLE

High Seas & High Stakes Series

HIS LADY SMUGGLER

HER GENTLEMAN PIRATE

HIGH SEAS & HIGH STAKES - BOOKS 1-2 BUNDLE

Daughters Of The Gods Series

BANISHED-GUARDIAN-FALLEN

DAUGHTERS OF THE GODS - BOOKS 1-3 BUNDLE

Stand Alone Books

TO SIN WITH SCANDAL

OUTLAWS

ABOUT THE AUTHOR

Tamara is an Australian author who grew up in an old mining town in country South Australia, where her love of history was founded. So much so, she made her darling husband travel to the UK for their honeymoon, where she dragged him from one historical monument and castle to another.

A mother of three, her two little gentlemen in the making, a future lady (she hopes) and a part-time job keep her busy in the real world, but whenever she gets a moment's peace she loves to write romance novels in an array of genres, including regency, medieval and time travel.

www.tamaragill.com
tamaragillauthor@gmail.com

Made in the USA
Monee, IL
04 October 2023